UNDENIABLE LOVER

A WARRIORS OF LEMURIA NOVEL #4

ROSALIE REDD

UNDENIABLE LOVER
A Warriors of Lemuria Novel #4

By

Rosalie Redd

For permissions contact: Rosalie@rosalieredd.com
Cover Design: Melody Simmons
ISBN: 9781944419189
United States of America

CHAPTER 1

Saar curled his fingers around the hilt of his sword and pressed his lips to the cool steel blade. The skin around his mouth puckered, a constant reminder of the age-old, disfiguring scar that tracked from his cheek to his chin. Hot and bitter, bile rose in his throat, and the mixture of sweat and frustration blended into a toxic brew.

Dampness coated his skin. He took a step forward, his boots sliding over the smooth, polished stone floor.

Sunstones lining the underground Keep's cave walls flared to life. The light reflected in his opponent's cold stare.

"Come now, I didn't expect you to beat around the bush. You can do much better." Saar's adversary smiled, and his blue eyes swirled with amber flecks. So familiar, so chilling.

The taunt sent a rush of adrenaline through Saar's veins. He tightened his grip around his favorite weapon and hefted the heavy blade. Focused on his rival, he waited for the slight flinch around the eyes, the tell-tale sign his opponent would attack.

…and there it was, the twitch under Noeh's left eye. With a quickness bred into his Lemurian blood, Noeh brought his short sword down.

The clash of steel ricocheted against the Keep's stone walls.

Blade pressed to blade, Saar's muscles strained under Noeh's pressure. Although they didn't usually spar with real swords, both Saar and the king were on edge. Sparring with authentic weapons provided the extra rush they desperately needed.

Noeh's mouth lifted at the corner. "Concede."

The demand lit a fire of conviction in Saar's chest. He shoved his sword harder against Noeh's, forcing the male to step back. "Never."

Noeh relaxed his grip and swiped his sword under Saar's blade.

Saar used the momentum to his advantage. He brought his blade around, and the tip scratched Noeh's ear. Blood pooled along the cut.

"*Craya!* That's twice now you've nicked me." Noeh drew his mouth into a thin line, his gaze focused on Saar's lips.

Saar lowered his sword in deference to his king. "Actually, that's three. Set and match."

Noeh sheathed his weapon and wiped his palm over his face. The red sunstone in his ring, the one that marked him as king, glittered in the light. "Not long ago that wouldn't have happened, at least not so easily. Damn my deafness!"

If Saar could've absorbed Noeh's weakness, taken away his pain, he would've done so without hesitation.

Everyone had a weakness that wouldn't heal. Noeh's were his ears. Saar—the scar that marred his face. He cleared his throat to dislodge the ache that had formed there. "Your Majesty. You are our king. I, for one, would follow you to the grave."

Noeh exhaled, and a sad smile tugged at his lips. "You are my most trusted, my most loyal warrior. You've proven that to me, time and again." His attention focused on Saar's scar before drawing to his eyes. "I couldn't have chosen a better Commander of Arms."

Noeh almost died because of you. Father's words echoed in Saar's mind, and the familiar guilt weighed heavily on his shoulders.

He glanced around the room, taking in the empty weights against the far wall and the sparring dummies lined up in a row. Pictures graced the walls, many of warriors in battle, some with swords raised above their heads, others in beast form, long hair coating their tall, muscular bodies, claws elongated, tusks protruding from their jaws.

Saar longed to shift into his beast once again, but he wouldn't take the chance, not unless he needed to protect someone he loved, like Noeh.

In recent memory, only two Stiyaha had returned to their human state—Tanen, the Keep's council leader, and Noeh, their king. How had they shifted back? No one knew for sure, but some thought it had something to do with their new mates.

Three dark bands circled Noeh's neck, the sign of an unusually strong bonding. Most bonded males received two bands and those who received one often wished they'd never mated.

Saar brushed his fingers over his throat. No mark would ever darken his skin. A longing deep inside twisted his gut into a tight ball, and he clenched his teeth.

Although the sac under his tongue had filled with his bonding ink a time or two, he'd never pierced the pouch. The liquid that would bind him to a mate and produce the bands remained intact.

Not that it mattered. There wasn't a female in the Keep who would have him. Over his five hundred and fifty years on this planet, a few had lain with him for the experience, but all recoiled at his disfigurement. Now, he kept his distance from all females.

He placed his sword in his scabbard and faced his king so that Noeh could read his lips. "I do what I was born to do, fight this war for you and Alora."

In this elaborate game they played on Earth, Gossum were the enemy, the ones to defeat in this bitter fight for the right to control the planet's water. The fate of humankind, oblivious and caught in the middle, rested on the war's outcome.

Unfortunately, the last battle hadn't ended well. A tic pulsed in Saar's jaw.

Noeh narrowed his gaze, flecks of amber sparking in his eyes once again. "Speaking of the war, seems Zedron has some new players in the game. A new enemy for us. Perfect, just what we needed." He pursed his lips, the pink of his skin lightening from the pressure.

"Where do you suppose those shape-shifting bears...the Ursus came from and why hasn't Alora, our illustrious goddess, mentioned anything about them to us?"

An unbidden image flashed across Saar's mind. During the last battle, a young Ursus female, mace in hand, stood before him ready to attack. She had long hair as dark as night, braided in a tight plait down her back, golden-yellow trim interwoven between the silky strands. Resolve glowed in her eyes, and she'd attacked him with a ferocity he'd never seen in a female before.

Although she was his enemy, he couldn't bring himself to harm her. A strange desire to touch her skin had flitted through him, and before he could stop himself, he'd trailed a finger down her soft cheek. His fingers tingled at the memory.

"Saar?" Noeh's voice broke through Saar's thoughts, pulling him back to the present.

"Your Majesty?"

Noeh paced to a rack of barbells, leaned down, and placed his hands over the heavy weights. The muscles in his arms bunched beneath the similar military-issued black shirt all the warriors wore. He tapped his ring against the metal, once, twice, three times. The ping echoed through the empty room. "You didn't answer my question. Where did the Ursus come from and why hasn't Alora said anything?"

Saar pulled a toothpick from a small pocket under his belt and twirled it between his lips. The ragged tip caught on the soft tissue of his inner lip, scouring the flesh. Blood, tangy and bitter, filled his mouth. He waited to reply until Noeh turned around. "I have no answer for you on the bears or Alora. It doesn't matter. In the end, we will prevail."

The lines around Noeh's eyes softened. "Your faith never ceases to amaze me and is only rivaled by your loyalty. Yes, my friend, we will succeed. We have to..." he blinked and peered at his ring. "I don't know what I would do without Melissa and Anlon. If I ever lost my son..." His jaw tightened.

Saar tugged the dagger from his belt clip, and ran the sharp edge over the jagged toothpick. A few shavings curled into a tight twist and slid to the stone floor. "Melissa would tell you not to invite trouble."

A short, stifled laugh emerged from Noeh's lips. "She'd tell me to get on with winning this war." He smiled and streaks of amber flashed through his eyes. "Put together a scouting party. Locate Mauree's hideout. With all those troops, she can't be that hard to find. We need to locate her before she attacks again."

Saar sheathed his dagger, returned the toothpick to his pocket, and bowed. On his shoulder, his marking for loyalty burned while the ones for courage and honor were eerily silent. A sense of pride lightened Saar's chest for his three dark, jagged lines. Born with his own unique marks at birth like all Stiyaha males, he'd honored his values well over the years and the markings had never faded. "Yes, Your Majesty. We leave at nightfall."

Saar's mind drifted to the beautiful female. Nothing good could come from seeing her again. She was the enemy. By all rights, he should kill her. He ground his teeth.

I pray I don't find her. Yet, a part of him deep inside wanted nothing more.

CHAPTER 2

*K*aelyn placed her hand against the sliding glass door. The cool surface was a welcome balm against the heat radiating from her skin. Through the lake house's window, the mid-afternoon sun reflected off the patio chairs, gleaming with a brightness that hurt her sensitive eyes.

Birds chirped, and a chipmunk skittered over the deck, stopping to pick up a bread crust hidden under one of the chair legs.

The sudden urge to chase the small animal away, warn it of the danger close by, rippled over her skin. Her inner bear grunted in frustration. She was a shape-shifting Ursus warrior in a horrific war over Earth's water. *Run, little creature, run.*

Familiar footsteps tapped across the linoleum floor. The scent of licorice filled her senses. *Theron.*

He approached her from behind and wrapped his arms around her in a close hug. The short sleeves of his dark T-shirt hit mid-bicep, pulling tight over his firm muscles. "Tell me, favorite niece, what ails you?"

For a brief moment, she leaned into him, soaking up his strength and his warmth. He was the only one she allowed such close, intimate contact. Yet even with him, she kept the walls high around her heart.

She turned in his embrace to study him.

Lines formed around his eyes, echoing the pain harbored in their deep brown depths. Her chest constricted for him, anguish and self-loathing filling her to the brim. She couldn't maintain his gaze or stand to receive his comfort any longer. Instead, she pulled away then padded to the kitchen island, eager for the barrier between them.

He drew his mouth into a frown. "Spit it out, sweet pea."

"I *hate* this war." Spittle flew from her mouth, and she fisted her hand so hard, her nails dug into her palm. "I'd rather fight against the Gossum than with them."

He strode to the opposite side of the kitchen block and placed his hands on the surface. The muscles in his shoulders stiffened. "I agree, but we don't have a choice. The game has shifted. We fight for Zedron now."

Kaelyn's claws elongated, and she swiped her hand against the pans hanging from the ceiling above them. A loud clatter echoed off the tiled walls and stainless steel appliances. With a long, curved handle, a metal ladle fell and jangled against the countertop's stone surface before landing on the floor. The lone relic seemed out of place, and a stab of kinship with the utensil hit her in the chest.

"...and Mauree. She's using you—"

"Kaelyn..." Theron held up his hand. He peered over her shoulder.

"—to get to me. Stop protecting me. I don't need or want your help."

"Did I hear my name?" Mauree's smug voice snaked into the room.

The hair on Kaelyn's nape rose. She turned to face Mauree, her former enemy, now leader.

Mauree wore a tight-fitting blue tank top over a short mini-skirt. Her long, elegant legs ended in a pair of pink high heeled shoes, a bow gracing the top of each. The sweet adornment was in contrast to her abrasive personality.

"My, my, fancy finding the two of you here. Splendid. That makes my job all the easier." Mauree smiled, revealing a perfect set of white teeth. With her blonde hair and blue eyes, she was the epitome of beauty, but her aura was pure menace.

7

Blood pounded at Kaelyn's temple. Unable to resist the urge to fight, she bolted toward Mauree and grabbed her arm. She slammed the other female against the cold steel fridge. Kaelyn raised her hand, eager to slice one of her sharp nails across the female's throat.

As if held by an invisible force, her arm seemed frozen in mid-air.

As much as she wanted to kill Mauree, she couldn't. When Zedron had obtained the Ursus from Alora in the war, he'd programmed them with the inability to harm Mauree. Smart move on his part as taking another opponent's players in the game could be risky. Loyalty was hard to ensure. His protection was the only thing keeping Mauree alive.

Theron gripped Kaelyn's shoulders, and he yanked her away from her true enemy. He wrapped his arms around her in a giant bear hug, holding her in place. She strained against his grasp, but he held on to her. Teeth gnashing together, she grunted, the sound turning into a snarl.

Mauree slid her hands down her skirt, straightening out the wrinkles. She patted the sheathed dagger strapped to her thigh. "Tsk, tsk, dear. You know better than that. You can't hurt me. Besides, I've added a little protection, just in case."

She meandered over to Theron and ran her fingers over his shoulder, stopping at the edge of his T-shirt. With apparent intimacy, she trailed her nail over Theron's exposed bicep.

Goosebumps visibly formed on his skin. A warning chuff burst from his lips.

Mauree laughed, the sound grating on Kaelyn's nerves. "You'll come around. You always do."

Kaelyn's bear roared inside, eager to thrash, rip, and shred her nails into the female. "Leave him alone. He doesn't want you."

"Kaelyn, enough." Theron's breath tickled her skin as he whispered in her ear. "Remember, keep your friends close, but your enemies closer."

She struggled against him, but he refused to let her go.

Mauree chuckled. "Oh, I beg to differ. He pretends to resist, but he can't hide how much he wants me. Enough of that, though," she waved a hand in the air, "I want to inform you both of a change in plans."

Theron released Kaelyn.

After backing up, she scooted out of his reach. His constant need to protect Kaelyn burned like a lit coal in her gut.

He crossed his arms over his chest. "We're listening."

Mauree tittered. "The battle at Roan's Rock was a huge success. We took down several of Noeh's warriors—"

"But he got away." Kaelyn couldn't resist the jab, eager to injure Mauree in any way possible.

Mauree's smile faltered. Her blue eyes flecked with gold. "It's only a matter of time before he's dead. But that's not what I wanted to talk to you about. Zedron expects results...and soon. We lost a few soldiers in the battle, including Jakar. So, I no longer have a first lieutenant."

"Oh, how sad." Kaelyn smiled.

Mauree narrowed her gaze. "Indeed, it was as you shall soon see."

A smug smile tugged at Mauree's lips, and she turned to Theron. "You will be Jakar's replacement, leading both the Gossum and Ursus armies."

His stoic features paled. He glanced at Kaelyn. "She is the rightful Ursus heir. Arbane and Entrania were her parents. I cannot—" He clamped his lips shut.

Rage, deep and powerful, raced through Kaelyn like lightning. Against her leg, the spiked ball of her mace dangled from her hip in its protective leather case, the weight familiar and welcome. She wrapped her fingers around the handle.

Visions of bashing Mauree's head with her weapon raced through her mind. The evil female had killed Kaelyn's parents. Mauree deserved nothing less than death.

"That's what makes you perfect for the job, Theron. This way, I know both you and Kaelyn will comply. The other Ursus will fall in line." Mauree chuckled.

Kaelyn blinked. A scream bottled up inside. *No...* Theron hated this war as much as she did, hated fighting for Mauree. It would turn his soul black to lead her army. Yet, he would do anything Mauree asked to protect Kaelyn.

Kaelyn's pulse pounded at her temple. She focused her attention on her uncle. "Don't you dare, Theron. I will never forgive you."

Over five hundred years ago, her brother, Noden, had sacrificed himself to save her, abandoning her in the process. She wouldn't lose Theron as well. Bitter and cold, self-loathing coated her insides.

A small flinch flitted over his features, but that was the only indication her words had hit their mark. A tic pulsed to life on his cheek. "I do this for you, sweet pea."

"Perfect." Mauree clapped her hands. "Prepare a few troops for a little scouting adventure come nightfall, but first there's something we need to do." Mauree trailed a fingernail along Theron's chin, a seductive smile forming on her lips.

Without a word, he followed her from the room.

A scream burst from Kaelyn's throat. Her claws elongated, digging into one of the kitchen cabinets. Small shavings drifted to the floor, eerily similar to the tears streaking down her face.

CHAPTER 3

aelyn crept over the rock, her hands gripping the rough edge. Eyes narrowing, she surveyed her surroundings. Trees blended into the dark forest. A light mist traveled between the old growth sentinels turning them into macabre creatures with long pointy nails, not unlike her new partners, the Gossum.

She clenched her jaw and took a deep breath. Salty and cool, the cleansing air was a welcome relief, and she closed her eyes to enjoy the momentary reprieve.

The familiar, clipped tone of Theron's whistle pierced the air. She tensed.

They weren't alone.

She gripped the whistle dangling from the chain around her throat, her fingers trailing over the hand-carved bear's head and brought it to her lips. With practiced skill, she placed her fingers over the holes in the bear's ears and blew. The shrill tone of her reply echoed into the night.

She slid down the rock's slick surface and landed on a pile of ferns. The fronds bent under her weight. Silent and quick, she padded between the trees, her fingers loose around the handle of her mace.

Through patches of fog, moonlight sliced between the trees,

providing enough of a glow to catch shadows moving in the distance. A Gossum. Once human, the creature's bald head, now devoid of hair, shined in the moon's rays. With pointed claws and a long barbed tongue, the ugly creature slinked further into the forest. She curled her lip.

There were five members in tonight's unit, two Gossum and three Ursus, including her uncle Theron and herself. Their assignment—search for Alora's troops along the coast.

Damp. Dreary. Dismal.

What a wet mess. *Thanks, Mauree.*

That was how the bitch doled out punishment. Kaelyn clenched her jaw. So be it.

A twig snapped.

Screeee...

The eerie cry sent a shiver over Kaelyn's shoulders.

From behind a tree, a large male raced toward one of the Gossum, his sword raised above his shoulder. Because of the dark clothes he wore, she tracked him by the moonlight glinting off the blade. He moved with a swift, silent grace. A tendril of respect for her enemy churned in her gut.

No matter. She had a job to do.

On quiet feet, she pursued the male, her unrelenting need to battle for her god, Zedron, urging her forward.

The Gossum hissed, the sound snaking between the trees like the mist. He extended his claws and launched himself at the intruder.

Kaelyn drew closer. She yanked her mace from her belt.

Nearer now, the male's form became clear. Tall and broad, he wore dark pants, boots, and a dark shirt, golden armbands gracing his forearms. Beneath his shirt, his muscles flexed as he moved. With the ease of a trained warrior, he sliced his sword across the Gossum's arm.

The creature howled in pain. Blood spurted from the amputated end.

The Gossum snapped its long tongue at the male's face, but he jerked in time to avoid the barbed tip, angling toward her.

She got a good look at him. Brown hair, cut short around the ears, accentuated his strong jaw and chiseled face, but couldn't hide his most striking feature, the scar that ran from his cheek, over his lips, and down his chin.

It's him. The male who touched me.

Kaelyn stopped in her tracks. The mace grew heavy in her hand.

As if her fingers had a mind of their own, they traced a path down her cheek, just like he'd done during their last battle.

Her pulse quickened. Heat raced up her neck.

Rage… Desire…

The conflicting emotions spurred her forward. She twirled her mace.

With one quick thrust, the male scored the tip of his blade deep into the Gossum's chest. The creature stilled then slid to the forest floor in a pile of black sludge.

She attacked, the whoosh of the mace her only warning.

He blocked her blow with his sword. His gaze narrowed then widened.

For the briefest moment, Kaelyn thought she saw a spark of something in his eyes. Relief? Happiness?

No. How could that be? He was the enemy…wasn't he?

She glanced at his fingers curled around the hilt of his sword. Rough, strong, steady.

Her chest tightened. Deep inside, she longed to feel his touch once again. How long had it been since she'd allowed a male to touch her that way? Decades.

Surging anger sent a rush of hot adrenaline to her muscles. Using the energy, she cried out and swung her mace at his head.

He blocked her blows, again and again, but never attacked her, only defended himself.

"Fight, damn you!" She hurled the words at him.

"Tell me your name."

She swung at him again and missed. Not possible. She was an excellent warrior, one of the best in her Tribe.

Maybe he was just that good. *I hope so.*

Her breath caught in her throat at her errant thought. He was the enemy. He needed to die.

She whipped her mace over her head. He held her fixated, his blue eyes swirling with bits of amber. *So beautiful...*

He thrust his sword, catching the chain in her mace.

Her weapon flew from her grasp.

Faster than she would've thought possible, he yanked her arm behind her and pinned her to him back to front. The tip of his blade lay against her throat, his arm resting between her breasts.

"Tell me your name." His breath cascaded over her throat, warm and demanding.

She squirmed in his embrace, but all she did was rub against the hard planes of his chest and abdomen. The bare skin on her arms prickled from the friction.

He tugged her closer against him. His scent of pepper and lime infiltrated her senses, sending a heady rush of desire through her. She quivered in his arms.

"I'm not going to harm you." His voice was low, controlled.

That he thought she shivered from fear sent a new round of anger into her bloodstream. She renewed her efforts to free herself. Elongating her claws, she tried to scratch him, but he had her pinned, and her claws scraped the thin air between them. Any closer and she'd snag his balls.

Her mind wandered to places it shouldn't go, like what it would feel like to cup him in her palms.

She cried out in frustration.

"This is the third and last time I'm going to ask you this. Don't make me ask again. What is your name?" Despite his threat, his tight grip was warm and comforting. He could kill her in a heartbeat, yet, he hadn't.

The question burned in her mind. "My name is Kaelyn. Why haven't you killed me?"

"Kaelyn, Kaelyn." Her name rolled off his tongue, deep and sensual.

She wanted to hear him say it again. Irritation beat in her chest, fluttering like a trapped bird. "Let me go."

He removed the tip of the blade from her throat and spun her to face him. "*Craya*. What do you—"

She slapped her open palm against his cheek. The sound of flesh hitting flesh echoed in the space between them.

He narrowed his gaze. His cheek reddened, and her attention drew to his scar. "Take a good long look." The set of his jaw was dark, predatory.

She refused to look away. Instead, she raised her chin. "I'm not afraid of you."

Amber flecks swirled in his eyes intermixing with the blue. "You should be."

She wasn't. He'd been too gentle. His words didn't match his actions.

Theron's frantic whistle pierced the air. The message was clear—run.

She didn't hesitate. With a quickness born of her species, she morphed into her bear, clothes disappearing beneath her fur. She bolted through the trees, eager to put distance between herself and this male that had unbalanced her with his touch, his voice, and his deep blue eyes.

Against her better judgment telling her not to glance behind her, she couldn't stop herself.

He was in hot pursuit, her mace clasped in his grip.

Damn.

Her only hope—outrun him.

Saar's pulse pounded. He pursued Kaelyn through the forest. The memory of her at the battle at Roan's Rock haunted him night and day. While trapping her in his embrace, his fingers had caressed her soft skin and they twitched with his need to touch her again.

He jumped over a fallen log, and his boots squished into the moist earth. The earlier mist cleared, revealing bright moonlight. Soft and enticing, the moon's rays penetrated between the trees, lighting up the path. The route she took headed toward the ocean. He needed to catch her before she arrived and escaped him.

What he'd do if he caught her again, he wasn't sure. She was the enemy. By all rights, he should've killed her when he'd had the chance.

He clenched his jaw.

Another mistake? Just what he didn't need. He was racking those up like they were pieces of excrement stuck to his boots. Doubling his effort, he plunged through a patch of thick blackberries, the dead vines catching on his pants, his shirt, his bare skin. He didn't care.

Another blemish wouldn't change anything. His scar said it all. As much as others heralded him for his tenacity, skill, and leadership on the battlefield, he wasn't perfect and that stuck in his craw.

When she'd glanced at his scar, he'd goaded her, trying to fill her with unease at the grotesque blemish. Kaelyn hadn't looked away. A tightness wrapped around his chest, squeezing the air from his lungs.

His concentration drew to his target. Her dark fur blended in with her surroundings, but with his night vision, he spotted her movements with ease. She slowed and raised her head. Her snout quivered as if she scented the air. Soft grunts burst from her, and she increased her pace.

Encumbered in his human form, he didn't give up. There was no way he'd shift into his beast. He refused to take that risk.

Moonlight shone through the trees. Only a few yards in front of him, Kaelyn was almost to the cliffside.

She skidded to a stop and swiveled to face him. A few small stones slid over the edge and pinged against the rocks. Waves crashed below.

Saar stepped from the trees. His boots crunched against the tiny pebbles that littered the moist dirt.

Still in bear form with dark fur and long claws, her breath eased from her mouth in puffs of steam. She lumbered to and fro, assessing him.

"Kaelyn…" What could he say to her? They were enemies. He swallowed the bile that rose in his throat.

She stood on her hind legs, jagged claws extending from her front paws. A low chuff eased from her lips. A warning.

16

Before he could think better of his decision, he tossed her mace on the ground at her feet. "Your weapon. Now, we're even."

Morphing into her human form, her clothes reformed onto her body. Dressed in a tight-fitting dark shirt and black pants, she was tall, built strong and tough. Luscious, with curves a male could get used to touching, she bent down to pick up her mace. Her focus never leaving his, her brow furrowed. "Why would you return a weapon to your enemy? I'd never make that blunder."

A mistake… Her words hit home harder than he cared to admit. Not wanting her to know how much she'd affected him, he smiled. "I rather like your spunk. You're fun to play with."

"Yeah, right." She twirled her mace above her head, the spiked ball whooshing through the air, faster and faster.

Raising his sword, he prepared to defend himself. His heart beat with anticipation. He looked forward to stripping her of her weapon once again.

Kaelyn scrunched her brows. Perfect and full, her lips pouted as she focused on him. The sudden urge to wrap her in his arms and kiss her overwhelmed him.

He lowered his sword.

She blinked and lost control over her mace. It twirled in a strange arc, as if it had a life of its own. Unable to maintain her balance, she took a step back. The weapon tore from her fingers, soaring over the abyss behind her.

"Wait! Stop!" He shouted.

Her foot slipped. She fell. A scream ripped from her throat.

Saar launched himself at her, arms outstretched.

Her fingers clawed at the small tufts of grass lining the edge of the cliff then she disappeared over the side.

His stomach heaved into his chest. He was too late.

She was gone.

He rushed to the edge and looked over the rim.

She lay against the boulders at the bottom of the cliff, arms and legs sprawled over the rocks at odd angles.

She's alive. Relief flitted over his nerves.

If she'd died, she would've turned to sand. In the battle at Roan's Rock he'd killed an Ursus, and the bear had turned to sand like a Stiyaha not sludge like the Gossum.

She's not the enemy. She can't be. He wouldn't believe otherwise.

A new resolve built in his chest. "Hold on, Kaelyn. I'm coming."

CHAPTER 4

Saar scrambled down the side of the precipice. Bits of rock skittered under his boots as he half-slid, half-ran down the mountain. His chest tight, he glanced toward the once-spunky Ursus female. Sprawled against the large boulders, her twisted, broken body lay motionless.

"Goddess, Alora, please let her live." His prayer was but a whisper, caught in the swirl of wind raging around him.

On the ground at last, he clambered over the boulders, the sharp edges digging into his palms. A wave crashed against the large reef. Spray rained down on him, drenching him in an instant. The salty tang of seawater coated the back of his throat.

Saar reached her, his gaze raking over her body. Forcing down the fear that threatened to overwhelm him, he used his warrior training to assess her injuries, to determine the best course of action.

She lay on her back on a flat portion of rock, her hips wrenched to one side, her shoulders the other. Her face was away from him, covered by the thick wrap of her braid. There was no blood that he could see. A choked breath heaved from his throat.

He knelt at her side, his knee resting next to her thigh. The carved likeness of a bear's head dangled from her neck on a small woven chain. He placed his finger alongside her throat, between the chain's fine links. Beneath his fingertip, her pulse beat.

Relief skittered over his nerves.

With a gentleness he didn't fully understand, he moved her long, thick braid away from her face. The soft, fine strands teased the pads on his fingers. A bit of golden material intertwined between the locks was a beautiful addition.

He focused his attention on her features. Dark lashes, lush and full, graced her cheeks. Soft and smooth, her unblemished skin was a shade darker than his. Her lips, oh, those plump, puckered lips, begged for his kiss.

"You're not my enemy." The words tumbled from his lips. Speaking them aloud reaffirmed his belief that she couldn't be his opponent. Yet...she'd fought with the Gossum, fought against him.

A rush of heat ran from his chest down his arms.

Friend or foe?

She was an enigma, and he had to know the answer.

"Kaelyn, wake up." He gently shook her shoulder.

She didn't stir.

Another wave crashed against the boulders. Water trickled over his boots and around her body.

The tide was coming.

He didn't have much time. If he didn't move her, she'd drown.

There was no time to worry about broken bones. With great care, he slid one arm under her knees and another under her shoulders then cradled her against his chest. Her braid whacked his collar bone before landing in the space between them. Its softness teased the skin on his bicep, and he wanted to unravel the fine tresses, see the long strands free from their bondage.

Another wave brought more water, this time rising half way up his calf.

The waves now covered the small bit of beach he'd crossed before climbing the rocks. The other direction was no better.

He'd have to scale the cliff.

It would be treacherous, but it was either that or swim to the beach with her in his arms and hope the tide didn't drag them out to sea.

He stood, pulling her tighter against him.

"You! Stop!" The wind whipped the words, swirling them around Saar's head.

He glanced in either direction, but saw no one.

The hair at his nape rose.

He slowly raised his head and peered toward the cliff's top. Perched on the edge was a tall male. He had shoulder-length brown hair that blew in the wind. With eyes to match, the resemblance to Kaelyn was unmistakable. *Kin...*

"Let her go," the male rasped.

Saar's inner beast growled. A possessiveness he didn't understand ripped through him. "No. She's mine." The words melded into his chest, setting up home as if she belonged to him. Confusion swirled in his mind, but there was no way he'd give her up, not now.

He glanced at her. "Guess we're going for a swim."

Before he could change his mind, he ran across the boulders as fast as safety allowed. At the end, he jumped, holding on to Kaelyn for dear life.

Saar landed in the water feet first. His boots hit the sand. The pull of the surf tugged him backward. He fought to maintain his balance, clutching his precious cargo against his chest.

She didn't stir.

A tendril of fear snaked into his mind. How bad were her injuries? What if she never woke up? *I have to get her to Gaetan.* The old *Haelen* would heal her.

The ocean's mind-numbing cold seeped into his muscles, slowing him down, but he slogged through the swells until he was close enough to run along the shore. Increasing his pace, he emerged onto the beach.

Movement out of the corner of his eye caught his attention. The male on the bluff ran down the same slope Saar had taken earlier. He hefted a mace twice the size of Kaelyn's.

There wasn't much time.

"Rin, open a portal." Using his mental connection to the gateway, Saar called to the little Jixie that manned the Keep's Portal Navigation Center.

"I hear ya, Saar. Homing in on yer location. What...what are ya doin' on the beach?" Rin tsked. *"Locked in. Opening in five, four..."*

Not far away, a mist coalesced near a stream that poured over a small waterfall into the ocean. The fog swirled into a ball, faster and faster. An opening appeared in the middle. The walls of the Keep appeared on the other side, and Rin stood over the *Porte Stanen* and the sunstones that ignited the portal.

With Kaelyn in his arms, Saar ran toward home, safety, and hopefully, answers.

CHAPTER 5

*A*lora hurried to the baskets of newly arrived produce. It wasn't often Lemuria received a shipment of fresh produce from the Andolin star system, so she was fortunate to make it here before the large crowds gathered. She snatched a Kollo fruit and glanced at the other shoppers. Situated among the uppermost branches of a Rolmdew tree, Lemuria's open-air market buzzed with activity. In the early evening, customers hurried to obtain the fresh fruits and vegetables before they ran out or the market closed, whichever came first.

Not wanting to take the time but unable to resist, Alora brought the Kollo fruit to her nose, closed her eyes, and inhaled. The sweet, delicate fragrance was a reminder of what they no longer had on Lemuria—the ability to grow enough crops to support their population.

She clenched her fist and juice from the Kollo fruit dribbled down her fingers. Her planet was slowly dying.

Earth, the pretty blue orb in a solar system with a single sun, contained the one ingredient Lemuria needed more than anything—water. The much-needed liquid would not only sustain crops, but would help quench the fires that raged during the summer months.

A sense of urgency rippled along her nerves. She needed to hurry home so she could visit Noeh on Earth, tell him about the Ursus, friends turned enemies. This was something she should've done already, but hadn't had time.

Close by, a female with a scarf covering her head and shoulders shoved a handful of berries into her basket, her movements quick, hurried. The ends of her blue hair poked from beneath the material and the orange spots on her arms indicated she was an Arotaar.

Dressed in a fine tailored suit, the male next to her frowned, his eyes narrowing in distaste. He shoved her out of the way. She stumbled and lost her hold on the basket. The berries tumbled to the wooden platform.

Alora's pulse spiked. "Hey! Watch it!"

The male glared at her. "What's your problem? She's a slave, and—"

Alora stepped into the male's personal space. "Everyone deserves respect."

He raised his chin and flicked some imaginary lint from his custom-made silk jacket. "Not everyone."

A bitter taste filled Alora's mouth. The Kollo fruit slid from her fingers and landed on the wooden platform with a soft, squishy plop. "It's Lemurians like you that give our planet a bad reputation."

"Other species in the galaxy fear us. We should enslave every planet we come across." He tugged on the collar of his jacket.

"The slave faction should be abolished. If I had my way—"

"You free faction groupies are all alike. Save the poor, helpless people on other planets. Bah!" He spat on the ground, his saliva soaking into the dry floorboards. "At least the council keeps a level head."

The council. Some days she despised the council members, even though Radnor, her father-in-law, was their leader. If there was a dispute over a planet, the council intervened, as they had with Earth. Alora ground her teeth. "The council does its best to—"

"Enough." He shoved her aside. "I have better things to do than argue with the likes of you."

Heat flared up her face and into her cheeks. She stepped into his path. "What did you say your name was?"

He blinked then cleared his throat. "Get out of my way."

Seeing him squirm sent a rush of satisfaction through her. She smiled. "Be careful what you do and say. You never know who may be watching."

With a quick glance, he scanned the area then hurried on his way.

"Have a good evening," she called after him.

The female he'd pushed gathered the last of her berries, her fingers stained with the fruit's juice. Using the table for support, she pulled herself to her feet.

A pang of empathy hit Alora in the chest. She approached the female and placed a hand on her shoulder. "Excuse me. Are you all right?"

The female turned around.

Alora inhaled. "C...Carine. I didn't expect to find you here."

Carine lowered her eyes. "Alora, thank you for chasing away that male. Please, you should go. If Zedron found out I spoke to you..."

Zedron. At the mention of his name, Alora's stomach cramped. He was her rival in this war over Earth's water. She wanted Earth to become a free planet and barter with the humans for their precious resource. He wanted to enslave the humans and take the water by force.

Alora swallowed as she studied the young female. "Carine, has Zedron...has he...harmed you?"

She shook her head.

The bonds around Alora's heart loosened. She let out a quick breath. "You know I'm here for you if you need me. Come visit any time."

Carine's gaze rose to meet Alora's. Hope, fragile and small, reflected in her eyes. "Really?"

Alora placed her hand over Carine's. "Of course. Actually, I'd like that very much. I recently lost a good friend..." *Bellamy.*

Memories of the last time Alora was with her best friend flitted across her mind. The suspension bridge...the rhondo beast...Bellamy falling to the planet's surface...her screams...the crunch of bones.

Hot and fast, tears stung Alora's eyes.

Carine touched Alora's arm. "I'm sorry for your loss. I'd like to be your friend, very much."

A new companion was just what Alora needed, and her chest swelled at the Arotaar female's offer. "You know where I live, right?"

"Yes, Zedron showed me your place once." She bit her lip and looked away.

Alora frowned. "Of course he did. Say," Alora glanced around, searching for Zedron's familiar shoulder-length dark hair, "I thought he didn't allow you out on your own. Did something change?"

"He gives me brief allowances away for shopping and chores." She held up her bracelet. "My arm band has a timer. If I'm not back before the credits run out, he'll—" Carine clamped her mouth shut, cutting off her words.

Alora fisted her hand, her rage building beneath her skin, hot and fevered. "I hate everything about slavery. I'd free you in a heartbeat if I could."

Carine nodded. "I'd like to visit you, but I'd have to be careful. Zedron can't know. I think I could squeeze in some time away without him finding out."

"I wouldn't do anything to jeopardize your safety. You're welcome to stop by, but you'll have to come at night. I'm not home during the day." *No, lucky me. I'm cooped up in my solitary dark room when the sun is out.* To make matters worse, her characters suffered a similar fate, unable to handle the sun's rays without burning to death. *Damn sanction.*

"Zedron told me about your and Veromé's punishment for cheating in the game." The lines around Carine's eyes softened. "To be apart so much must make it tough for you and your mate."

Alora's thoughts drifted to Veromé. A pang tightened her chest. *My mate, my love.* "Yes, it does. Our time together is limited to sunrise and sunset. If anything happens during the day, you can always go to him."

"Thank you." Carine smiled, creases forming around her eyes.

Alora wrapped her hands around the Arotaar female's. "I'm so glad I ran into you. Please, come by soon."

Carine's bracelet vibrated, the tremor pulsing through their connection. She tugged her hands away and glanced at the display. "I have to hurry home and check in. Thank you."

Carine bowed her head once then fled toward the cashiers.

Alora's pulse sped. "Damn you, Zedron."

She peered into the night sky, the stars sparkling between the Rolmdew's branches. Somewhere out there was a little blue planet, one that held the key to helping Lemuria. The war raged, and she needed to visit Noeh, soon.

CHAPTER 6

*S*aar's boots clicked against the stone floor in perfect rhythm with his pounding heart. What had he done? He'd brought his enemy into the Keep, his kind's innermost sanctuary. This couldn't end well. Yet, he didn't regret his decision.

He glanced at the infirmary's closed wooden door. *She* was in there. "Kaelyn."

The word echoed off the corridor walls, and the sunstones embedded in the rock flared to life. The Keep, ever aware of its inhabitants, reacted to their emotions. Warmth emanating from the gems cascaded over his skin, but didn't alleviate the nervous energy coursing through his veins.

He pulled a toothpick from his pocket and shoved it into his mouth. The sharp end stabbed his cheek. Bitter and warm, blood coated his tongue. *"Craya!"*

Noeh's familiar gait reverberated down the corridor. The shadowy bulk of his figure moved with the grace and power only the king possessed.

Saar removed the toothpick and gave his friend a quick bow. "Your Majesty."

Noeh's stare bored into Saar. The fatigue rimming his blue eyes was the new norm for the king. Running the Keep with a toddler in the family wasn't easy.

"Rin tells me you brought a female into our sanctuary. An Ursus female. Why?" His sharp, demanding tone left no room for argument.

Saar straightened his shoulders. "I have no satisfactory answer."

A tic pulsed in Noeh's jaw. He studied Saar for a moment then ran his hand through his hair. "If you were anyone else, I'd—"

"Put me in the dungeon for insolence."

A brief smile tugged at Noeh's lip. "Ah, *craya*, you know me so well. You must have a reason. Tell me."

Saar twirled the toothpick between his fingers. What could he say? *I'm attracted to her? I couldn't resist her charm? No.* Not appropriate. He didn't understand his reaction to Kaelyn. Instead, he glanced at the infirmary door. "I neglected to tell you earlier, but I don't believe the Ursus are our enemy."

Noeh blinked. His mouth pursed. "How can you say that? They killed some of our warriors."

Saar focused on his friend. "In the battle at Roan's Rock, I slew an Ursus and it didn't disintegrate into black sludge. Instead, the dead soldier turned to sand. Just. Like. Us."

Noeh studied Saar, his attention flitting back and forth. He glanced toward the infirmary. "This female...tell me what happened."

"This female," *Kaelyn*, "fell over a cliff, landed on the rocks along the shoreline. She was unconscious. I brought her here straight from the Portal Navigation Center." Saar's gut twisted, a mixture of fear and confusion roiling together into a noxious blend. He shouldn't care, but he did.

Noeh placed his hand on Saar's shoulder. "You just about gave Rin a heart attack. When I received the message traveling through the sunstones along the corridor, his message was a jumbled mess." Noeh's eyes shimmered with flecks of amber. "I never doubted you had a good reason, my friend. You, I trust with my life."

Saar's throat constricted, and he gave his king a brief nod. "Sheri's in there with Gaetan. He said he'd let me in as soon as they've had a chance to examine her."

"I'm placing you in charge of this...prisoner. Once she wakes, interrogate her. Find out what you can about her, the Ursus, and their connection to Mauree. If she's not bedridden, put her in a stronghold cell. Until we know more, she is the enemy."

Noeh's command crept inside Saar, swirling and tightening around his chest. The dark line for honor on his shoulder flared to life as his resolve to please his king solidified. When they were both youths, he'd saved Noeh from a Gossum, but not before the creature had scratched the deep wound in Saar's face and left Noeh in a coma for a week. If only Saar hadn't convinced Noeh to stay after class to watch the bucks fight in the woods.

"Noeh could've died because of you. Does your loyalty lie with the future king or yourself?" Father's words, and the guilt that accompanied them, echoed in Saar's mind.

"Saar, did you hear me?" Noeh gripped Saar's shoulder. Worry lines formed around his eyes.

A rush of heat seared Saar's ears. "Say again?"

"You left me there for a moment."

Saar grimaced, his scar pulling tight against his skin as he relived the memory of his father's verbal blow. He wouldn't share his thoughts with his king, not on this topic. "What was it you needed?"

"Gaetan could be a while, so I'm leaving this situation in your capable hands. When I left my chamber, Melissa had her arms full with Anlon. He's crawling all over the place, getting into everything. If I don't help out..." Noeh ran his palm over his face, the red sunstone in his ring catching the light.

Saar raised his hand. "Say no more. I'll report to you as soon as I hear."

"Thank you, my friend. I couldn't have asked for a better Commander of Arms." Noeh clapped Saar on the shoulder then headed down the corridor the way he'd come.

As he disappeared from view, Saar's determination to please his king solidified in his chest. Best friends since childhood, their trust in each other had never wavered.

CHAPTER 7

"*D*id you get the blood sample?" Gaetan stood from his worn wooden stool, and the old lumber creaked as if relieved from bearing his weight. Pain, his constant companion, wormed into the joint at his knee, settling in for another splendid round of torture. He secured his grip around his staff, using the ancient wood for support.

Sheri hadn't responded to his question, so he glanced at her. Shoulder-length blonde hair cascaded around her shoulders. She stood beside the new arrival, the female Ursus, who lay supine on one of the infirmary's stone-carved beds. With an intensity in her hazel eyes, she held up a needle, deep red blood filling the tube. "Got it right here."

"Excellent. I'll analyze the enzymes for compatibility with—" He sucked in a breath. Pain rippled down his leg, and he leaned against his cane. The orange sunstone at the tip brightened, the heat warming his palm. A gift from his sister Ginnia long ago, the sunstone was a constant reminder of her love for him and his duty to her.

"Gaetan?" Sheri padded across the room, her soft-soled shoes skating across the polished stone floor. She gripped his elbow, but he shook her off, unwilling to receive support from anyone.

"I'm fine, Sheri. Thank you for your concern." He smiled, letting his natural ability to calm others filter along their connection. "My leg just fell asleep there for a moment."

Before he could stop himself, his attention tore to the beakers, bottles, and assorted medical paraphernalia scattered across the shelves lining the infirmary's walls. He focused on one bottle in particular—the one that contained his pain killers.

Relief. That's what he needed.

He hobbled over to the counter, aware of Sheri's assessing gaze. Appearing as nonchalant as possible, he wrapped his fingers around the container. With a quick twist, he released the cap, shook one of the pills into his palm, and popped it into his mouth.

He swallowed the tablet dry.

Ah, much better.

Sheri placed the vial with the Ursus female's blood into a rack next to an old medical text. The solitary tube's dark red color gave him pause. A shiver, part hunch, part dread, skittered over his nerves. The blood seemed more like their own than that of the Gossum.

"Gaetan, are you sure you're okay?" Concern filled Sheri's voice.

He turned to face her. "It's been a long night. I'll need to rest my leg soon."

Yes, the deformed piece of meat he called a leg couldn't withstand much weight. When he was younger, the pain hadn't been so bad, but over the past few hundred years, the agony had increased. Now, the bitter ache was a constant in his life.

Sheri crossed her arms. "You work too hard. Let me handle the analysis on that blood, okay?" The compassion in her hazel eyes spoke volumes.

He sighed. "That would be nice. Thank you."

Sheri set out a glass slide and picked up a jar of solution. Using metal tongs, she gripped a clean cloth, dipped it into the concoction, and then wiped the solution over the slide. She glanced at their patient. "She looks so peaceful. Do you think she's the enemy?"

The female's dark braid hung over the side of the medical bed, the tip almost touching the floor. Thanks to the sunstones and their healing ability, they hadn't needed to remove her clothing to heal her wounds. With closed eyes, her pale skin glowed with a soft innocence, reminding him of his sister, Ginnia.

She was locked away in a cell in the strongroom for releasing the traitorous Mauree. Noeh hadn't wanted to jail the Keep's seer, but she'd admitted to the crime. Unwilling to let anyone else care for his sister, Gaetan had vowed to watch over her.

He exhaled. "I trust Saar's judgment."

"I hope you're right." Sheri nodded toward the Ursus female. "Despite her innocent look, she's a warrior. I'd hate to be on the receiving end of her wrath."

"Point well-taken." He glanced at Sheri, but he focused on the cabinet behind her. Beyond the glass door, wrapped in a brown cloth, the blue sunstone of legend sat in the uppermost corner of the top shelf. After Sheri had retrieved the sacred stone from Mauree, Noeh had placed the ancient relic in Gaetan's care—to watch over, keep hidden. Sooner or later, he'd have to get rid of that thing. The blue sunstone was more trouble than it was worth.

The sudden urge to take another pill flitted over Gaetan's nerves. His fingers twitched.

Goosebumps rose along his arms.

He returned his attention to Sheri. "Thank you for assisting me with our...," his attention flitted to the female, "...guest."

Sheri smiled. "Of course, my pleasure. I enjoy helping you in the infirmary. It gives me a chance to give back, use my medical training to aid you and the warriors here."

Mated to Tanen, Sheri had been turned from human to Dren and was now a vital part of the Keep. She picked up the vial with the female's blood and twisted the lid. With careful attention, she tilted the small bottle. A single drop slid from the vial and landed on the glass slide.

Gaetan placed his hand over Sheri's arm and gave her a gentle squeeze. "Your assistance means more to me than you know."

Each day his pain worsened, and he was glad for the reprieve she offered.

"Results?" he asked.

Her eyes widened. "As I suspected from the color, Lemurian blood, like ours. What do you think this means?"

He stifled a laugh. There wasn't anything funny about this war, this battle for Earth's water. Yet, circumstances had veered into the macabre. Telling friend from foe wasn't as easy as it once was.

"What a tangled web we weave." He peered at the ceiling. "What's going on, Alora?"

Silence.

He shrugged. Not that he'd expected an answer from his goddess, but he longed for a response all the same.

"Let's check our patient one last time before we let Saar in, shall we?" He hobbled over to the Ursus female, relying on his cane more than he cared to admit.

Sheri beat him there. She placed her fingers against the female's wrist. Her brow knit together. "Heartbeat seems normal. Shouldn't she be conscious by now?"

"The brain is a mysterious organ. You never know what will trigger a response." He gripped the edge of the sheet and pulled it up to the female's shoulders. Leaning over, he patted her on the arm. "We've done all we can, my little patient. The rest is up to you."

CHAPTER 8

The creak from the infirmary door echoed into the corridor. Saar turned around, adrenaline spiking in his veins. "Is she all right? Is she awake?"

Gaetan stood in the entryway. His features were drawn, lines pinched into the skin around his eyes. The old Haelen held out his hand. "Please, enter and see for yourself."

Saar didn't hesitate and strode toward the door. The sunstones lining the corridor brightened, as if the Keep sensed the tension in the air.

As he crossed the threshold, his attention drew to Kaelyn. Looking peaceful and out of place, her motionless, supine form rested on one of the medical tables. Only her head and shoulders were visible, the rest of her was hidden beneath a thin sheet. Saar's inner beast growled, the sound loud in his ears.

Gaetan spoke, but his words seemed distant, masked by the roar in Saar's head. He ignored the healer and proceeded to Kaelyn's side.

"What's wrong with her?" He clenched his jaw.

"Nothing, as far as we can tell." Sheri pushed away from the counter and approached. She tucked a lock of hair behind her ear and smiled. "Since you know her, maybe you can bring her around."

If that were so, this would've been easier. He preferred running on logic over instinct. After a quick exhale, he cleared his throat. "I don't know her. All that matters is she was injured. I couldn't leave her behind."

Gaetan's cane ticked against the stone floor as he approached. He placed his hand on Saar's back. "Well, she's a mystery that's for sure. Her blood test indicates she's Lemurian, related closer to you and me than her Gossum cohorts."

Her long, dark lashes graced her cheek, accentuating her fine, perfect skin. His fingertips itched and his hand jerked. He curled his fingers into a fist, fighting the need to touch her.

"So, she's healed?" His voice broke on the last word.

"She had several broken ribs, a cracked vertebra, and a punctured lung. The sunstones healed her, but she'll need time to rest, recoup from her ordeal." Gaetan wandered to his stool, his gait more pronounced than normal. With a soft sigh, he sat on the worn edge.

Saar pulled the toothpick from his pocket and shoved it into his mouth. He rolled it around with his tongue, using the familiar movement to calm his nerves. "Why isn't she awake?"

Sheri removed her smock and tossed it into the hamper in the corner. "That's the question of the hour, isn't it?" Her gaze flicked from Saar to Gaetan. "Unless you need me for anything else, I'm going to meet Tanen in the Hall of Scriptures. He wants my help searching the ancient texts for any information about the lines in my palm."

She held up her hand, palm out. Etched in the middle was the distinct imprint of the English letter "M," the symbol for Lemuria. It had appeared after she'd transitioned into a Dren. Only she and Queen Melissa had such a mark. Noeh had commissioned Tanen, the Keep's council leader, to search the ancient texts for anything he could find on it.

So far, they hadn't had any success.

"Thank you for your help, Sheri." Gaetan smiled in his comforting, healer's way.

Sheri crossed the infirmary and shut the door behind her. The latch's soft click echoed in the quiet room.

Saar returned his attention to Kaelyn. Her long braid, dark and silky with hints of golden-yellow from the interwined cloth, hung over her shoulder, nearly touching the floor. Before he could stop himself, he trailed his fingers over the fine lock, pulling it into his palm. The pads in his fingers tingled, and a low, needful groan escaped his lips.

"You okay there, big guy?" Gaetan's voice cut through the fog in his brain. A knowing smile tugged at his lips.

Kaelyn's braid tumbled from Saar's grasp, and the back of his finger grazed against her arm. "Yeah, I'm good."

Kaelyn's mouth parted. She audibly inhaled, her chest rising beneath the sheet. Her eyelids fluttered open. Hazel-green, the color of the mountains, her eyes focused on him.

She stiffened. A cry of pure frustration, fear, and anger burst from her lips.

Before he could speak, she scrambled from the medical bed. The sheet caught in her legs, and she tumbled to the floor.

$\sim$

Kaelyn fought the fear coursing through her veins. She'd lingered below the surface, bits of words, smells, and sounds melding into a cacophony of senses, consciousness close, but just out of reach. That was, until an electrical current of energy against her arm had thrust her up and through the confusion.

Her first vision—the tall, muscular male who'd pursued her through the forest. *Saar.* The images raced through her mind—the cliff, shifting back to human form, her foot slipping...the fall.

She thrashed with her feet, caught in the sheet and the undertow of emotions.

Hands, strong and warm, gripped her arm, her leg.

Fighting harder, she kicked with her foot. Her heel connected with something hard, yet giving.

A loud, deep male groan rumbled through the air. The sound

37

crawled into her chest, working into her senses, calming her. *No.* This wasn't right.

With a quick push, she scrambled to her feet. Unfamiliar surroundings—medical beds, counters filled with bottles, beakers, equipment. A male, unmoving, sat on a nearby stool, a cane gripped in his palm. He had short brown hair, a lock of gray at his temple. His eyes sparkled with mirth.

Nothing looked familiar.

The air in the room seemed hot, stifling. Sweat coated her arms.

The tall, muscular male she'd seen before rose from the floor. Blood trickled over his chin. He gripped the bridge of his nose, and with an abrupt twist, popped it into place. A sharp inhale like a hiss escaped his lips.

"Kaelyn, I won't hurt you." His words were rough, no doubt due to his wounded pride.

Good. She extended her claws.

The idea to shift flitted through her mind, but she didn't know where she was. Freeing her bear here would only confuse her creature. Instead, she lashed out with her hand, swiping her claws dangerously close to his face. The horrific scars indicated she wasn't the first to attack him that way.

A growl, low and menacing, burst from him. "Stop, before you hurt yourself."

She laughed. "Me? Seems like you're the one who's injured."

His brow furrowed over his blue eyes, and the warmth in their depths seemed to call to her on a level she didn't understand. Butterflies swirled in her stomach. Using the energy coursing through her veins, she launched herself at him.

He met her halfway, grasping his fingers around her wrist with one hand. Using their combined momentum, he tugged her toward the wall and flipped her around at the last moment. Her heart skipped a beat.

With a gentleness she hadn't expected and one she didn't deserve, he pressed her against the wall, cradling her in his embrace. She couldn't move, yet he didn't hurt her. Instead, his warmth seeped into her skin, lighting up the nerves along their connection.

Against her will she responded to him, her pheromones secreting her sweet pea perfume into the air. Heat flushed her face, fueled as much by her anger as her desire for him.

He tensed. His large body pressed into hers—powerful, intimate, enticing.

She whimpered in frustration.

"Shh…shh…you're safe here. No one will harm you. You have my word." His gentle lilt penetrated into her psyche.

Fighting him still, she squirmed against him, not ready to give up.

His strength, his scent, his touch worked their magic, pestering her, tormenting her…teasing her.

At last, she couldn't take anymore. Tension drained from her muscles. A sense of relief washed over her, spurning her frustration and confusion.

"Let me go." She spat the words at him, but they didn't contain any venom.

He pulled back enough to look at her. Her reflection glimmered in the depths of his eyes. It seemed as if he could see into her soul.

His brow rose. "You won't kick, bite, or scratch me? Because I'm not letting you go unless the answer is 'no.' Don't worry, I won't hurt you."

He seemed so sincere. She wanted to trust him.

After a long few seconds, she shook her head.

A small smile tugged at his mouth. His scar stretched the skin into a bizarre grimace. Despite his disfigurement, or maybe because of it, something in her chest fluttered. He was a warrior just like her, broken and damaged. The only difference—her scars were on the inside.

When he released her, cool air replaced his warmth. She shivered, and her chest constricted at the lack of contact. She fisted her hand, her claws digging into her palm.

"Well, Saar, seems you have things under control. Time for proper introductions." The male on the stool smiled. He glanced at her, his blue eyes swirling with bits of gold. "My name is Gaetan. Nice to meet you, Kaelyn."

She pursed her lips. "Why am I here? What do you plan to do with me?"

He chuckled. "Saar, I'll leave that for you."

Her gaze tracked to the counter behind him. Nestled between a couple of small beakers and an assortment of bottles lay her bears-head whistle, the cord dangling over the counter's edge. She inhaled and clamped her hand to her bare throat. Not since she and Noden had carved the matching set had the special calling device not dangled from her neck. She even bathed with it. A sense of nakedness and loss constricted her chest.

She held out her hand. "Give me my whistle."

"No." Saar's mouth twisted into a scowl.

Anger, dark and fast, rippled through her. The thought to battle him once again flashed through her mind.

Gaetan stood. He wobbled for a moment then steadied himself with his cane. "My leg needs a rest. I'm heading to my quarters."

Saar's brow furrowed. "Are you sure you're okay? You seem—"

Gaetan waved his hand in the air as he strode to the door, his movements slow, yet determined. The cane tapped along the stone floor. "I'm fine. You have your hands full with our...guest."

Heat raced up Kaelyn's chest and into her face. "I'm a prisoner, aren't I?"

Gaetan opened the door. A loud squeak issued from the hinge. He chuckled. "Saar, she's all yours. Good luck, my friend." With that, he strode over the threshold and disappeared from view. The sound of his cane tapping echoed down the hallway.

She turned to face the male who'd captured her. Crossing her hands over her chest, she glared at him. "Are you going to answer me?"

He laughed, a good hearty chuckle. "You're a feisty one, aren't you?"

She narrowed her gaze, heat rising to her cheeks once again. "You have no idea."

He pulled a cord from his belt. The woven braid shimmered in the light. "You're a prisoner of war. I'll answer what I can of your inquiries, but not until I know you won't run."

She glanced from the rope to him. "You wouldn't."

He smiled and damn if she didn't like the gleam in his eyes. "We can do this the easy way or the hard way. Your choice."

She bolted for the counter, unwilling to leave without her whistle. He tackled her from behind. She fell, her knee crashing against the stone floor. Pain raced up her leg.

He landed on her, pressing her face to the ground, but he didn't crush her with his weight. Instead, he cradled her against his body, preventing her from moving, his arms and legs wrapped around her. Self-hatred for getting caught so easily burned in her gut.

"That's what I thought, the hard way." He wrapped the silver rope around her wrists. Bound, she couldn't break his hold.

"I want my whistle!"

"Too bad."

"You think a rope is going to hold me?" She squirmed against him.

He chuckled. "Indeed, it will. We soak the rope in special, magical herbs. You can't shift, and the bindings will remain until I release you." He hauled her to her feet and pulled her to him, her back pressed against his strong chest. With a soft push, he urged her forward.

Good thing, she'd enjoyed the warmth of his skin far too much.

CHAPTER 9

$\mathcal{M}$auree woke from the best dream of her life.

Visions of Theron with his dark, haunted eyes drifted through her mind. Damn, he was sexy. She tried to hold on to the image, but the harder she tried, the faster the dream escaped her grasp. With a deep groan, she shoved her face into her pillow. Was it really time to wake up?

She inhaled, and Theron's spicy licorice scent filtered into her lungs. Ah, the dream was more than a fantasy. She grinned and stretched. Her muscles ached in all the right places, bringing back pleasant memories from their earlier encounter.

More, I want more.

She brushed her fingers over his pillowcase. The fabric was still warm from his skin, but he was gone.

She opened her eyes and sat up. The brilliant light of late sunset penetrated through the window, lighting the dresser with its huge, carved wooden frame in shades of amber and gold. In the mirror, she caught a glimpse of her reflection.

Hair tousled around her shoulders, lips red and swollen, she looked like a female who'd enjoyed a good time in the sack. Happiness and pride rippled through her. She smiled and winked at her image. "You're beautiful, baby."

She peered at the closed bathroom door, her euphoria deflating. "Theron?"

Silence.

Hairs along her nape rose. She stuck out her bottom lip.

The bathroom door opened, the slight creak of the hinge ringing in her ears.

He strode into the bedroom, a towel wrapped around his waist. Her attention drew to his six-pack abs and the fine hairs that ran under the towel's edge. She had the sudden urge to tug the material free and expose his large package hidden beneath. Her fingers twitched.

"Ah, you're back." She poked her legs from between the sheets, showcasing her best attribute.

His attention drew to her bare flesh before pulling to her eyes. He shrugged.

He ran another towel over his head and dried his hair. The muscles in his shoulders and arms flexed with his efforts, bringing back memories of his strength and stamina.

She sucked her bottom lip between her teeth and gnawed on the tender flesh. With dramatic flair, she patted his empty place on the bed. "Come, we still have time before the troops head out."

His jaw clenched. He didn't look at her. Instead, he grabbed her brush off the vanity and pulled the bristles through his hair.

She fisted the sheet between her fingers. "Theron..."

The muscles in his shoulders tensed. He tossed the brush onto the dresser. The handle bounced against one of her perfume bottles. The vial rattled, teetering on the edge of falling, before righting itself once again.

"I don't have time for games. Kaelyn...that *Kasard* Stiyaha captured her." He wheeled to face her. His mouth drew into a thin line, and a tic pulsed in his jaw. "I will find her."

Mauree slid to the edge of the bed and stood. Using the sheet as a makeshift dress, she tugged the material around her midriff. She ran her fingers down Theron's arm. "Are you sure about what you saw?"

A low hiss eased from him. "Yes. A large male with a scar across his face held Kaelyn in his arms. He took her through a portal. I couldn't stop him…"

"That was Saar." She trailed her fingers over his shoulder in small circles.

"If he kills her, I will torture him until—"

"Don't worry. If he'd planned to kill her, she'd already be dead."

After a quick turn, she paced to the window. The sun was down. Darkness crept through the trees, claiming the territory as if it had every right. Which, of course, it did.

The sound of rustling clothes caught her attention.

She peered at Theron.

He tugged a pair of dark jeans over the taut, firm muscles in his buttocks. Damn, he looked yummy.

"Mmmmm, Theron. You know how to tease a girl. Perhaps we should—"

The temperature in the room dropped several degrees. Goosebumps rose on Mauree's arms.

A light blue mist slid through the slight opening in the window.

Mauree held her breath.

Theron turned to face her. "What's going on?"

She swallowed past the lump in her throat. "Zedron." His name came out on a squeak.

The vapor grew, coalescing in size and shape into a tall male. The form solidified.

Zedron wore a dark tailored suit with diamond cufflinks and a handkerchief dangling from the coat's breast pocket. He smiled, revealing a perfect set of white teeth. Somehow, the gleam didn't quite make it to his eyes. Instead, they were cold, hard, assessing. His gaze raked down Theron then focused on Mauree.

She cleared her throat. "Z…Zedron. So good to see you. What brings you here?"

"A status update. You had an…*opportunity*…to kill Noeh. Yet, he still lives." Zedron's words were low, controlled. If he'd said them any quieter, she wouldn't have heard him. The ease in his voice chilled her, and she pulled the sheet tighter around her waist.

Remembering their first encounter together, she knew better than to show weakness to her boss. She raised her chin. "The battle at Roan's Rock was a rousing success. We took out several of Noeh's warriors, weakening his position in the game—weakening Alora."

His lip twitched. "I'm listening."

She glanced at Theron. The hard lines in his face bolstered her conviction. If Zedron killed her and sent her back to the character board on Lemuria, then so be it. Might as well go out big. She crossed her arms over the bed sheet. "You could learn a little patience. Be happy with our progress."

Zedron's face reddened.

This was it. He'd kill her or let her get on with her business. A tremble started in her knee. She stiffened her leg, forcing herself to remain calm.

The lines in Zedron's face softened ever so slightly. A soft chuckle eased from his throat, building in tempo and volume until it turned into a full-blown laugh. The mirror shook within its frame.

Mauree exhaled.

Zedron's chortle subsided, and he wiped his eyes with the back of his hand. "Unexpected and unpredictable. I like that about you. Well done...for now. But, I expect you to handle Noeh and soon. Understood?"

"Of course. My goal hasn't changed. Eliminate Noeh and the rest of Alora's troops will run around like chickens with their heads cut off. I *shall* succeed."

He nodded, and a streak of silver flashed through his blue eyes. "Very well. See that you do." His fixating stare tracked to Theron. "A bit of advice. Don't let...distractions...get in your way."

She stiffened. "You needn't worry. I'm focused."

He gave her one quick nod, his stare locked onto her. "Ensure that remains so."

Before she could respond, he transformed into the blue mist. The vapor slid through the small opening in the window and dissipated into the night.

She closed her eyes and prayed she could live up to her bravado.

CHAPTER 10

Kaelyn woke with a start. Pin prickles crept down her arm. How long had she slept? Her pulse sped. Locked in her cell carved into the Keep's bedrock, she had no way to know. It could be night or day. She rose from the lumpy bed and paced the small space between the bars of her cell and the wall.

This far underground, the scent of wet stone and dampness permeated everything, soaking into her skin, chilling her. Through force of habit, she brought her bound hands to her chest, searching for the comfort of her whistle. Her fingers grazed against bare skin.

She inhaled.

Searing rage burned through her veins, bubbling to the surface in a scream so loud the sound reverberated off the walls. Out of frustration, she tried to morph into her bear. The bindings around her wrists sparked with an eerie iridescence.

She remained in human form.

A tendril of fear weaseled into her chest, sprouting roots, growing like a weed. She fought against the rope with all her might, letting the frustration fuel her efforts. Again and again, she tugged, pulled, and fought, until her energy waned.

Even with her inner bear's strength and toughness, she failed.

47

She wrapped her fingers around the bars. The cool metal was a welcome reprieve on her hot and sweaty palms. There was no way she could stay here. Who knew what they would do to her.

Another round of panic released a fresh supply of adrenaline into her bloodstream. She tightened her grip on the bars and yanked. Her muscles shook, straining with the effort. The bars were as immovable as the male she'd met...Saar.

A bead of perspiration dripped from her brow and landed at her feet. The drop darkened the stone floor, wiping away some of the dirt and grime that had collected over the ages.

She pushed away from her unrelenting cage and sat on the edge of the worn and tired cot. Across the corridor, a tall female stared at her with sullen, forlorn eyes. Bits of her brown hair stuck out from her head at odd angles, and she crouched behind the bed, as if scared of the creature in the next cell—her.

"You can't get out, not that way." The female's voice was sweet, child-like. She had a much nicer bed, one with a soft, thick comforter, a small table and chair, and several old tomes scattered about the room.

Kaelyn stepped to the bars, curiosity getting the better of her. "Why not?"

"The Keep won't let you." The female's gaze darted to the ceiling before returning to meet Kaelyn's. "Don't worry. You won't be here long." The innocent look on the female's face broke down Kaelyn's resolve.

"I'm sorry if I scared you. My name is Kaelyn. What's yours?"

The female studied Kaelyn for a moment then emerged from behind the bed. She twirled a strand of hair between her fingers. "Ginnia."

The female had an air of innocence, and Kaelyn couldn't help but smile at her. "It's nice to meet you, Ginnia."

Ginnia gripped one of the bars and placed her forehead against the iron gate. "You shouldn't try to shift in the Keep. It's forbidden. Some of the Panthera do it, but they shouldn't."

"What?" Kaelyn blinked. "Why is it forbidden to shift?"

"Don't you know?" Ginnia scrunched her nose. "Be...cause..." her word came out in a sing-song tone, "the Stiyaha's beastie takes over, and they can't change back. Too many died trying. Noeh said no more shifting."

Kaelyn's thoughts returned to the battle with Saar. He hadn't shifted, not once. When he'd thrown her mace at her feet, she hadn't understood why, but this made more sense...and explained his words. *Now, we're even.*

"Noeh, he's your king, isn't he?" Kaelyn already knew that answer. He was the one Mauree was so desperate to kill, but she wanted to see Ginnia's reaction.

Ginnia's eyes softened. "I love Noeh. He was so sad when he put me here, but he had no choice. He is king after all, and I was bad."

Kaelyn flinched. So caught up in herself, she hadn't bothered to find out why Ginnia was locked up in a cell. "I can't imagine you did anything so wrong to lock you up. Why are you here?"

The unusual female kicked at a few small pebbles surrounding the bars that disappeared beneath the stone floor. "I let meanie Maureenie out of *your* cell."

Kaelyn inhaled. Her heart pounded double time. "You mean...Mauree?"

Staring at the ground, Ginnia only nodded.

That was unexpected. Kaelyn cleared her throat and spoke softly. "Why was she in a cell?"

Ginnia's focus returned to Kaelyn, her eyes flicking back and forth. "She tried to kill Queen Melissa when she was pregnant with Anlon." Her eyes brightened. "I love Anlon. I can't wait for him to get older so we can play together."

Kaelyn's scalp crawled. Mauree had tried to kill a pregnant female. Bile rose in her throat. If Kaelyn ever got the chance, she'd find a way to kill that bitch.

Ginnia leaned against the bars. "I don't want to talk about meanie Maureenie anymore."

Kaelyn flipped her braid over her shoulder and concentrated on Ginnia. "Okay, no problem. Tell me. What do you know about Saar?"

Something fluttered in Kaelyn's chest, and she mentally kicked herself for asking the question, but she had to know more about him, about this male that had brought her here.

"Saar is Noeh's best friend. He has an important job. He leads the warriors in battles. I like Saar. You do, too, I can tell."

Kaelyn backed away from the bars, putting distance between her and this strange female. "No. I don't."

She couldn't deny how he made her feel alive when she was with him, but she couldn't allow herself the luxury of developing feelings for a male she would one day kill.

Kaelyn paced in the small cell, her boots clinking against the stone floor.

"He will be your mate." Ginnia giggled, a soft child-like laugh. "You don't believe me, but you will."

Kaelyn swallowed then choked on her own saliva. Coughs wracked her body, over and over again until her eyes watered. She placed her fist over her mouth and patted her chest with her other hand. "That will *never* happen."

Over the years, a couple of males had shown interest in her, and she'd become intimate with one, but their relationship was short-lived. Afraid of losing them just like her brother, she wouldn't allow anyone to get that close again.

Ginnia's eyes flared, gold mixing with the blue. Her features softened. "We should be quiet now. He's almost here."

In the distance, the heavy gait of booted feet echoed down the corridor.

A shiver ran down Kaelyn's back, a mixture of anxiety, anticipation, and...desire.

The scent of pepper and lime washed over Kaelyn long before she spotted him. His familiar essence played havoc with her nerves, teasing her, luring her to press closer to the bars. Visible beyond the rods were only a few feet of carved stone wall.

Saar's footsteps increased in volume as he drew closer.

Her heart beat raced.

At last, he came into view. He wore a pair of charcoal slacks, black boots, and a dark shirt, the material snug over his muscular, well-defined chest. The gruesome scar across his face stretched tight across his cheek, dimpling the skin. He carried a tray in his hands, packed with an assortment of fruit, pastries, and two glasses filled to the brim with orange juice.

His focused attention was on the meal, his mouth pursed, as if working hard not to spill the liquid. He stopped and peered at Ginnia. "Good evening, Muzzie."

Ginnia pressed her cheek against the bars. She smiled, a grin forming on the side of her mouth not flattened against the steel frame. "Is some of that for me?"

The lines around his eyes softened. "Of course."

He glanced at Kaelyn. Gold flecks swirled in the depths of his blue eyes.

Her breath caught in her throat.

His gaze roamed her face as he assessed her.

She narrowed her eyes.

His lip twitched, and an amused smile tugged at the corner of his mouth, stretching the jagged scar that ran through both top and bottom lips.

After setting the tray on the stone floor, he picked up an orange juice and a muffin. Ginnia stuck her hands through the bars. She curled her fingers with impatience. "Me! Me! Me!"

"All right, Muzzie. Here you go." He chuckled and handed her the food.

She accepted what he offered and sat on her bed to eat.

Saar turned, holding up a muffin. Berries stained the dough in deep shades of purple and blue. Tiny bits of sprinkled sugar glittered on top.

Kaelyn's mouth watered for the wonderful sweet bread.

"Are you hungry?" His voice was low, steady.

The fruit's tart scent mixed with the warm baked goods. Kaelyn's stomach rumbled.

He chuckled, and the sound travelled through the space between them, cascading over her, tickling her ears.

She ground her teeth and tugged at the ropes once again.

"Taste it, Kaelyn, it's good!" Ginnia popped a bite into her mouth.

"I see you've met Ginnia, our seer." He held the muffin and the last orange juice just out of reach.

Her attention drew from the food to his eyes. Despite his scar, he was handsome with high cheekbones, a strong nose, and arresting blue eyes, ones that pulled her in against her will.

"I've met Ginnia." She had to force her tongue to form the words.

Ginnia popped the last of the muffin into her mouth, a satisfied grin on her face.

"You can take the muffin. It's fine, I assure you. If you were slated for death, you'd know." A hint of amusement flickered in his eyes. Saar held out the pastry, encouraging her to take it.

She slid her fingers between the bars as far as they would go and snatched the muffin from him. For the briefest moment, his fingers caressed hers. The warmth in his touch prickled her skin, and a shiver of delight raced down her back.

He held up the juice. "This, too." His gaze never leaving hers, he bent over and placed the glass on the stone floor within easy reach.

She took a bite of the muffin. The sweet taste ignited her salivary glands, making her jaw ache. Careful not to drop it, she placed the muffin on the bed. Kneeling on one knee, she drew the glass through the bars. With eagerness, she brought the lip of the mug to her mouth. Cool, sweet liquid slid down her throat. She almost choked and coughed against the back of her hand. "Why did you bring me this?"

He shrugged. "We might be enemies, but me and my kind, we aren't beasts."

She placed the glass on the floor, rose to her feet, and stared at him. "Aren't you? A beast..."

"Well, I guess we are at that." His smile returned. He dug his hand into his pocket and retrieved an object concealed in his fist. With deliberate ease, he unfurled his fingers. "Tell me about this."

Her hand-carved wooden whistle gleamed in his palm. She inhaled. Her hands jerked to her chest.

He tracked the movement. Amber flashed in his eyes.

She held out her palms. "Give it to me."

"So demanding." He tsked and leaned against the wall at the edge of her cell. Pinching the string between his fingers, he raised her whistle, tilting his head as if studying it. "From what I gather, seems whistles are a form of communication. How many different codes do you have?"

A twinge of anger rippled through her. Her whistle, along with her braiding scarf, were the only mementos she had of Noden. She kicked her glass of orange juice. The contents washed over the top of one of his boots, coating it with the sticky substance.

His jaw stiffened.

A small thrill of victory flitted through her veins. She enjoyed taunting him, getting a rise out of him, but she didn't want to dwell on the why.

He exhaled. "The questions will only get more difficult from here. Do yourself a favor and—"

"Kaelyn, you better do what he says. Saar's a big old cuddly bear, but don't make him mad. He's Noeh's bestest warrior."

A bear? Hardly. But she was well aware of his skill on the battlefield. Before she could stop herself, her gaze drifted south to his crotch. *I wonder if his skills in the bedroom match...* The wayward thought made her flinch. She wound her fingers around the cell bars, her knuckles turning white from the strain.

"You want this, don't you?" He dangled her whistle just out of reach.

Unable to grab her precious piece, frustration turned to grief and hot painful tears formed behind her eyes. She ground her teeth and blinked them away.

"Tell me something," he pulled a toothpick from his pocket and shoved the pointed tip between his lips, "if you fight for Zedron, why do you turn to sand?"

The small bit of muffin in her stomach hardened into a ball. She studied him for a moment. As much as she hated that they had switched sides in the war, she couldn't betray her kind. The less she told him the better. "That's how we've always departed this world."

The corner of his mouth rose, and a delightful dimple formed on his unblemished cheek. The little hollow was in such stark relief to his battle-hardened demeanor, she had to fight the urge to touch the small divot.

"I see." His blue eyes shimmered with determination, and he tugged the toothpick from his mouth. "Perhaps you'd rather answer a more pertinent question. Where is Mauree's hideout?"

Although he hadn't hurt her, she couldn't bring herself to trust him. He'd attack the lake house in a heartbeat, putting Theron and all her kind in grave danger. She wouldn't be responsible for any more deaths of those she loved. Pursing her lips, she pressed her forehead against the bars. "You'll have to torture me, and even then, you won't get that information."

Before she could react, he slid his hand between the opening, drew his fingers around her waist and pulled her against the bars. Pressed front to front, the metal rods between them, her senses went on high alert. Her hands wrapped around the bars, her face mere inches from his, her breath bottled up inside. So close he could kiss her, his eyes flicked back and forth as he studied her.

"I'm sure I could come up with all kinds of ways to torture you." His warm breath tickled her cheek, sending a thrill tripping down her spine.

"I'll bet you could." The words tumbled from her mouth without thought. Heat rushed up her throat and into her cheeks.

The yellow stones lining the corridor walls flared. Saar released her, and the sudden rush of cold air left goosebumps along her arms. She missed his warmth already. *Stop it!* She couldn't be attracted to him. Compelled by Zedron to fight against him, falling in love with him would only hurt her more.

Confused and uncertain, she turned her back on him. The rustling of his clothes filtered through the bars. When he didn't speak, she peeked over her shoulder at him.

He placed his hand against one of the stones lining the corridor. His brow furrowed in concentration, irritation flicking over his features. He glanced at Ginnia. "I'm sorry, Muzzie. I have to go."

Ginnia shook her finger at him. "Tell Noeh he can't ask too much of you."

Saar's Adam's apple visibly moved and one eyebrow rose. "Ginnia, you know I'd do anything for Noeh."

She smiled and sat cross-legged on her bed. "Bye, Saar."

He turned to face Kaelyn. His gaze raked over her—possessive, hungry, determined. "I'll come back soon, and we'll continue our conversation. That, I promise you."

As he walked away, his movement caused a slight breeze. Wrapped around one of the bars by its chain, her whistle fluttered in his wake.

Kaelyn gasped. He'd returned her precious whistle. A flicker of uncertainty beat against her resolve, and deep in the recesses of her heart, a part of her couldn't wait for him to keep his promise.

CHAPTER 11

*A*lora glanced at the Kollo fruit she'd left on the counter. Before she could visit Earth, she had to put away the produce she'd picked up at the market so it wouldn't spoil, but she couldn't resist the melon's sweet temptation. She grabbed a nearby knife and sliced into the rind. After putting down the blade, she picked up a single piece. One bite and then she'd visit Noeh.

A loud rap on the door echoed through the room.

Alora flinched. The melon tumbled from her hand into the bowl. With a forlorn glance at the fruit, she let loose a quick huff, placed the dish on the table, and headed toward the door.

"Coming!" Eager to visit Noeh, another delay wasn't what she needed.

She peered through the small hole in the door. Carine stood on the porch. Bathed in the lantern's glow, her features were drawn, lines forming around her eyes.

Alora's irritation faded. An ache built in the back of her throat. Carine had taken Alora up on her offer to visit, and despite Alora's need to hurry, she wouldn't turn her new friend away. She opened the door.

A rush of cool air filtered into the room, along with Carine's sweet scent.

"Carine, I'm so glad you're here. Come in, come in." Alora smiled at the young Arotaar female and gave her a welcoming hug.

She reminded Alora of her childhood friend, Etani. That's why Zedron had selected Carine as his slave, to hurt Alora. Hatred for him burned inside, churning a hole in her gut.

Carine pulled away. "Thank you...for letting me come here. I really wanted to see you."

Alora gripped her new friend's hand and gave it a gentle squeeze. "I'm so glad you did, but how did you get away from Zedron so quickly?"

"I'm to pick up some takeout from Janala's Place, his favorite restaurant. I'll claim they were busy. This gives us a few minutes together."

"Here, I was just about to have some Kollo fruit. Please, join me." Alora tugged Carine toward the couch.

The young female followed close behind, and they both settled onto the soft cushions. Carine focused on the melon, but didn't move to take any. Alora snagged a piece then scooted the bowl closer to her friend. "Please, have some. It's good."

After a long moment, Carine reached for a small slice and bit into the soft flesh.

Alora patted her new friend on the knee. "I'm so glad you decided to come over. What brings you by?"

"Are we alone?" Carine's attention wandered to the circular staircase, the one leading to Alora's bedroom. Tightness formed around her eyes.

Alora leaned forward. "Yes. Why?"

"I...have something for you." From between the folds in her shawl, she withdrew her hand. In her palm rested a small round disc in the deepest shade of blue.

Alora's heart skipped a beat then fluttered at breakneck speed. "That's a recording device from a visus bacin. How did you...," she inhaled, "...that's Zedron's, isn't it?"

Carine nodded.

"Why did you bring this to me?"

"There's something you need to see." She held out the device, urging Alora to take it.

Anticipation skittered over Alora's nerves like lightning. She grasped the small sphere, stood, and grabbed Carine's hand. "Come with me."

Alora padded across the smooth wooden floor to her scrying bowl. Situated near one carved wall, the water's surface glimmered from the room's overhead lights. With a quick flick, she dropped Zedron's device into the still pool. A concentric ring pulsed from the disturbance until the wave gently beat against the bowl's lip.

She glanced at Carine. "What will I see?"

The Arotaar female smiled. "Something that makes you happy."

"Wonderful. Let's do this."

She closed her eyes and inhaled, forcing her pounding heart to slow. Concentration was the key to unlocking the visions stored in the visus bacin. As per the rules of the game, she could only see her troops and the activities they performed. To get a glimpse of Zedron's army—a rare treat.

She moved her hands over the water's surface, slow at first, then faster and faster. An image appeared in the mist, slowly solidifying into Zedron's character board here on Lemuria.

The lights blinked, swirling around the map. Names graced each pinpoint of light...Mauree...Ram...Theron...one character after another. She glanced at the date stamp embedded at the bottom of the image. Two weeks ago.

She tapped her finger against the pool's edge. "I don't understand. Why am I seeing the character board?"

"Don't you see him?" Carine's voice held a hint of excitement.

"Who?" Alora refused to look at Carine for fear she'd lose the image.

"Weren't you sanctioned recently for, um, cheating?"

Alora ground her teeth. "I don't see what that has to do with anything."

Carine exhaled, the sound full of impatience. "You opened up that cave, saving Demir, who ended up killing Ram, right?"

"Ram." She'd seen his name. Her gaze flicked across the lights. Yes, there. Her breath caught in her throat. "Zedron, what did you do?"

She zeroed in on the light, bringing up Ram's history. His picture, along with his full biography, filled the scrying bowl. She scanned the record—Gossum leader, killed by a throwing star. The rest was blank. His soul should've appeared on the character board, ready for another war on another planet.

A sense of giddiness lightened Alora's mood. "Zedron, you dirty dog. I've got you now." She swiped her hand over the water, and the vision faded. "How did you find out?"

A mischievous smile tugged at Carine's mouth. "Zedron didn't see me watching him from the top of the stairs. He hovered over his visus bacin. When Ram didn't kill Noeh, Zedron threw him in a broken human body and returned him to Earth."

Perhaps this was the leverage Alora needed against her nemesis. "Zedron prevented Ram from returning to the character board after he died. That's against the rules."

"Yes, but Ram died, again. So, at least the poor guy made it there and is where he belongs."

Alora dipped her hand into the water and retrieved the small sphere. She held it up and peered at Carine. "May I keep this?"

"Of course. That's why I brought it to you." Conviction reflected in her gray eyes. "I'm taking a risk bringing this to you, but I despise Zedron as much as you do. Make him pay."

Alora wrapped her fingers around the recording device, squeezing the disc in her grasp. "Oh, he shall. He shall indeed."

CHAPTER 12

Saar stood outside the throne room's double doors. Noeh had sent a clear message along the sunstones, interrupting Saar's interrogation of the prisoner. *"Return to the throne room immediately."*

His pulse sped, and his thoughts returned to Kaelyn. The look of fiery determination in her eyes, the set line of her jaw, and her full, taunting lips haunted him still. He ground his teeth, the muscles in his jaw compressing to the point of pain.

Taking a deep breath, the Keep's age-old scent of stone and earth penetrated into his senses.

Calmer now, he shook his head and rapped his knuckles against the ancient wood. The twin doors opened without a sound, but the breeze they created caressed his cheek, teasing his scar, reminding him once again how he'd earned the jagged mark.

Jax, Noeh's personal attendant, motioned Saar forward. The tiny male's red hair bobbed around his head as he moved. "Oh, Saar, Noeh's expecting you. Indeed, he is. Come in, come in."

"Thank you, Jax." Saar patted the little Jixie on the shoulder and stepped into the king's throne room.

Saar scanned the area. Noeh wasn't alone. Queen Melissa, Prince

Anlon, and Gaetan were also in attendance, along with a handful of Saar's warriors. At his entrance, they all glanced his way.

Noeh rose from his chair. His blue eyes studied Saar before scrutinizing the soldiers. "That will be all. You're dismissed."

One by one, the warriors bowed low to their king before heading toward the exit. As the males passed Saar, each greeted him with a quick nod. Although they respected him, they kept their distance. His tough stance in war crept into his personal life. It wasn't only the females that avoided him.

The last to leave, Quentin gave Saar a wide berth. His attention flicked from Saar's silver emblem on his shirt to his eyes. "Commander."

Saar met the warrior's gaze. "Keep them in line, Quentin."

"Yes, Commander. Of course." His eyes beamed, as if he was eager to please.

Saar shrugged. Kill the enemy. Prove yourself in battle. That was all he cared about.

Jax closed the doors with a soft whoosh, exiting the room along with the warriors.

Noeh focused his attention on Saar. "What have you learned from the prisoner?"

The muscles in Saar's shoulders tensed.

Melissa clasped Noeh's fingers between hers. Her long red hair complemented the green in her knowing eyes. "You promised that would wait. Gaetan has news we all need to hear."

Gaetan cleared his throat. Seated in one of the chairs in front of Noeh's massive desk, he rubbed his knee. "Shall we wait for Demir?"

Noeh paced between the royal chair and his old wooden desk. He ran his hand through his hair. "No. The Panthera aren't available. He, Aramie, and some of his Pride are investigating a disturbance on the periphery of our territory, near a human town called Brinnon."

Anlon, the royal prince, tugged on the cuff of Gaetan's pants. Soft, golden ringlets curled around the toddler's ears. Gaetan picked him up and straddled the youngster's legs over his good knee. The child wrapped his fingers around the old Haelen's cane and studied the sunstone on the end with rapt attention. Gaetan was Anlon's guardian, as he had been with Noeh.

Noeh's attention focused on the old Haelen. "Tell us, my friend, what did you discover in Sheri's and Melissa's blood?"

A jolt of adrenaline pulsed through Saar's veins. Melissa and Sheri were the only two females in recent history that had survived the transition from human to Dren.

Gaetan bounced Anlon on his knee. The child's soft giggle filled the chamber. From across the room, a small ball floated through the air toward the young prince. When it was close enough, he wrapped his pudgy fingers around the toy. He'd inherited the levitation gift from his mother as all Dren received a special power. His skills continued to improve.

"You've got the touch, Gaetan. He always responds to you." Melissa smiled.

Gaetan bowed his head in deference to Melissa's soft, encouraging comment then glanced between Noeh and Saar. Lines formed around his eyes. "Sheri and I did several tests, but nothing seemed out of the ordinary until…"

Anlon squirmed in Gaetan's grasp and the old healer put him on the ground. The young child headed toward his mother.

"…we noticed something unusual. Seems they both have an extra enzyme in their blood. It's Lemurian based, but not Stiyaha."

Noeh exhaled. "What does that signify?"

Gaetan rubbed his knee. "I wish there was more to tell."

"That's it?" Melissa tugged Anlon tight against her chest. Her furrowed brow spoke volumes.

Saar wanted to rush into the infirmary and start performing his own tests, just to wipe that sad look from his queen's face, but he was a warrior, not a healer. He rapped his boot against the stone floor.

Gaetan gripped his cane, the dark lines of his marking visible beneath his cuff and trailing over the back of his hand. "We'll keep searching. Don't worry, I have faith we'll find—"

Blinding light lit up the walls.

A rush of air whipped through the room. Papers on Noeh's desk soared airborne, scattering about the chamber.

In the midst of the chaos, a solitary figure formed—Alora. She wore a shimmery white dress that changed color from red to green to gold when she moved. Her long blonde hair hung loose around her shoulders.

Saar bent to one knee and bowed his head in front of his goddess. His pulse raced with fear. Trouble came when the gods walked among mortals.

"Rise, my warriors." Alora's melodic voice filtered into Saar's soul, and he rose on command.

Alora focused on Anlon. A smile graced her beautiful features.

Saar had only seen his goddess once in his life, when she'd come to visit the Keep not long ago, telling Noeh he must bond with a female. Saar's chest constricted. Alora could easily demand the same of him. *No...please, no.*

She didn't look at him, instead her attention turned to Noeh.

The muscles in Saar's shoulders eased, at least for the moment.

"What do we owe the honor of your visit?" Noeh bowed his head, but his gaze never left Alora.

Her brows wrinkled, a pained expression crossing her features. "I bring news. None of it good."

Noeh pursed his lips. "Tell me."

She grazed her fingers over Noeh's cheek. "At least my decision to make you king was the right one."

Saar's pulse quickened. A nervous energy snaked into his legs, and he clamped down the urge to fidget. He wouldn't show unease in front of his goddess or his king.

Alora glanced to the others in the room then focused on Saar. The muscles in his chest squeezed so hard he couldn't breathe.

Her attention flicked to Noeh. "You surround yourself with those loyal to you. That is good. I fear you will need their help now more than ever." She raised her chin and took a large breath. "Other warriors were on their way here to help you in this war, but due to some unforeseen circumstances, your reinforcements now work for the enemy."

"Ursus," Saar blurted before he could stop himself.

Alora turned to face him. Her eyes flashed with silver. "Correct."

Noeh took a step forward, his face reddened. "Why?"

"I had to give them to Zedron, in reparation for…," Alora waved her hand in the air in a nonchalant gesture, but her jaw was tight, "…something I did. It was either the Ursus or the Stiyaha. Be thankful I didn't choose your kind."

Noeh wiped his hand over his face. "So, you're telling us not only did we lose an ally, we gained an enemy because you made a mistake? Beautiful."

Alora stared at him, and a strong gust of wind whipped through the room.

The sudden urge to put himself between his king and his angry goddess made Saar flinch.

Alora exhaled. "Noeh, I love you like a son. If you were anyone else…"

Noeh bowed his head. "Forgive me, Alora."

"Just know that the Ursus will kill you given the chance. Don't trust them." With that, she disappeared as quickly as she'd arrived. The breeze she left in her wake tussled Noeh's blond hair. His jaw stretched taut, and he glared at Saar. "Interrogate the prisoner once more then kill her, tonight."

CHAPTER 13

"*Interrogate the prisoner once more then kill her, tonight.*" Saar's knees buckled, and he placed his hand against the corridor's rough stone surface. His chest tightened, squeezing his lungs, his breaths shallow, forced. The sunstones lining the walls flared to life, warming the skin on his palm.

I have to kill Kaelyn.

His stomach heaved. The taste of bile filled his mouth.

He pushed off the wall and headed toward his destination. Heavy and firm, his boots clomped against the stone floor. His hand rested on the hilt of his sword, his trusty blade stored within its sheath. An image of him wielding his weapon through the air, the pointed tip slicing through—

The hair at his nape rose. Deep inside, a growl rumbled to life, low at first, but building with each heartbeat. His beast bucked against Saar's will, fighting for dominance. Pulling on his core values of courage, honor, and loyalty, he forced his inner beast to obey his command.

As much as the beautiful Ursus shifter tempted him, he couldn't go against his king's command.

Light from the stronghold and the cells within brightened the corridor.

He slowed his pace, and stopped just out of visual range.

A clink of glass against metal rang down the corridor.

"Saar, are you playing hide and seek with me?" Ginnia's gentle voice wafted from her cell.

A ball coiled in his stomach. What fate was in store for the little seer? Would Noeh command him to kill her as well?

He pinched the bridge of his nose. *Alora, please, anything but that.*

Numbness crept into his chest, erecting a barrier around his heart. He exhaled. Time to complete his task. He took a single step then another, his determination and loyalty to his king driving him forward. He couldn't bring himself to look at Kaelyn, so he glanced at Ginnia. "Hello, Muzzie. No time for hide and seek tonight, I'm afraid."

She pressed her bottom lip forward in an endearing pout and crossed her arms. "You're no fun. Kaelyn and I are bored."

Saar drew his gaze to the Ursus prisoner.

She leaned against the wall, one hand curled around the last bar in her cell, the silver rope entwined between her wrists. The bear's head whistle dangled from the woven chain around her throat, and her eyes gleamed with that spunky determination he'd already come to adore. Hardening his heart, he reinforced the walls he'd erected long ago. He couldn't afford to let his emotions interfere with his task.

He tracked his fingers to the hilt of his sword. The familiar sensation of the smooth metal should've been a welcome balm. Instead, the handle's coldness seemed like he'd shaken hands with dread. Goosebumps rose along his arms.

"Back for more?" The sexy tone of her voice poked at his walls, as if searching for a weak spot to gain entrance to his heart.

He glared at her. "I have more questions. Ones you *will* answer."

She pushed off from the wall and flicked her braid over her shoulder. The golden strand interweaved among the hair glimmered in the light. "We'll see about that."

Dressed in her tight-fitting dark shirt and black pants, the muscles in her shoulders and arms rippled with her strength. Saar perused her body, noting her full breasts and flared hips, but also her flat abdomen and the firm muscles in her thighs. She seemed like a female that could handle a bit of roughness in the bedroom.

He tensed at the forbidden thought. Heat crept up his back and warmed his ears. Not only would she reject him for his scar just like all the others, she was the enemy. Besides, she'd be dead soon…by his hands.

With more force than he'd intended, he growled at her. "Tell me about Mauree's hideout."

Kaelyn wrapped her fingers around the bars and leaned into the cage. Her cheeks pressed against the metal bars, her lips, plump and full, jutting between two rods. "No."

The sudden urge to wrap his arm around her and feel those luscious lips made him flinch.

A smile tugged at the corner of her gorgeous mouth. "Wow, you scare easily."

Searing anger rushed through his veins. Before he could stop himself, he acted on his desire, thrust his hands through the slits between the bars and tugged her to him.

Soft and warm, her curves melded against him, the bars captured between them. With a tenderness he hadn't known he'd possessed, he cradled her head in his hand.

She struggled for the briefest moment, then met his gaze. Her eyes dilated, and she slipped her tongue from her mouth, moistening her bottom lip. "Do it." Her words were breathless, husky, and all challenge.

"If you insist." He brought his mouth to hers in a bruising kiss.

Her lips were as warm and soft as he'd imagined. Bold and brazen, she licked the sensitive seam between his lips.

Craya, yes… He opened to her and their kiss deepened. Need, hot and fevered, raced to his groin. The sac under his tongue hardened as it filled with his bonding ink. His inner beast growled. *Mine…*

The muscles in her arms and back stiffened.

Saar released her.

She stepped away. Her trembling fingers rose to her mouth. In the lines etched around her eyes, confusion and…something that appeared to be revulsion. Those were reactions he'd seen on females before.

He curled his lip, the scar tissue pulling tight. Of course she'd rejected him. Yet, his bonding sac had hardened. In all his years, he'd never reacted to a female that intensely before. A tendril of foreboding crested over his shoulders.

"Are you two done?" Ginnia's soft voice filled the void.

Saar turned to the seer. "I'm sorry you saw that, Muzzie."

"I'm not." Ginnia snickered.

Kill the prisoner. Noeh's command beat at Saar's mind. His throat constricted, squeezing around a hard lump. There was no way he could kill Kaelyn in front of sweet, innocent Ginnia. *Craya.*

His attention returned to Kaelyn. She peered at him, her face a mask, her expression unreadable. Perhaps that was for the best.

He drew a key from his pocket and inserted it into the lock. With a quick twist, the heavy pad slipped to the ground. The fixture crashed against the stone floor.

He slid a finger around the cell's doorframe and tugged. A high-pitched squeak issued from the hinge.

Kaelyn's eyes widened. Fear, brief and swift, flitted over her features. "What are you…"

Grabbing her arm, he spun her around, pinning her to him back to front. With her hands bound by the rope, she was easy to capture. He wrapped her long hair around his fingers.

She gripped her hand over his, trying to free herself. "Let go."

"Take out your braid."

"What? Why?"

He glanced at the golden material interwoven among the long tresses. "I'm taking you for a little walk, blindfolded."

CHAPTER 14

Still in her cell, Kaelyn struggled, clamoring to free herself from Saar's grasp. She twined her fingers around his, her long braid caught in their combined grasps. "Let me go!"

"Stop fighting me." The muscles in his arms tensed, and he drew her tighter against him. She couldn't mistake the bulge in his pants pressing firm and long across her backside. Against her will her body responded, her pheromones sending the sugared scent of sweet peas into the air.

A low growl eased from his lips.

She continued to strain against his hold, and if she were honest with herself, it wasn't to escape him, but to revel in his scent, the warmth of his skin, and his overpowering strength. Frustrated, she threw her question at him. "Where are you taking me?"

"Out of your cell." His deep masculine voice tickled her ear, sending a shiver of delight down her spine.

"Why?" *To my death, no doubt.* She mentally shook herself. *Play along. This could work to your advantage.*

"That is all you need to know for now. Unwind your braid. I'll use," he rubbed his thumb over the material, the movement gentle, yet possessive, "your golden fabric as a blindfold."

She stiffened. A tendril of fear snaked along her nerves. "Blindfold me? Why?"

With a speed and grace she could admire, he flipped her around to face him. Hooded and tormented, his eyes flicked back and forth as he studied her. "Don't ask questions you don't want answered. Now, undo your braid, unless you'd rather I do it."

The idea of him releasing her hair, his fingers running through her long strands, sent a shiver of desire along her nerves. Enemy be damned, a part of her wanted him so very much. She bit her lip, and his attention riveted there. His eyes dilated, flecks of amber mixing with the blue.

"Fine." She pushed against him, and he released her.

Kaelyn tugged on the knot at the end of her hair and pulled the strands loose from the braid. The golden cloth, the one Noden had given her long ago, coiled in her palm. Saar's focused attention never strayed from her task, his gaze appreciative and almost reverent. His tenderness seemed at odds with his scarred looks.

A part of her wanted to understand him better, but the less she knew about him and his past, the better. Sooner or later, she'd have to battle him, and she didn't want any sort of caring or weakness to get in the way.

Done with her task, she handed him her braiding scarf. "I want this back. My brother gave it to me."

He studied her for a moment. "Noted. Now, turn around."

She wanted to shift into her bear, force her way past him, but even if she could, she didn't know her way around the elaborate tunnels and corridors in this place, this "Keep." She'd get lost for sure. With a quick exhale, she turned her back to him.

Saar placed her braiding scarf over her eyes and tied the ends behind her head. His touch was gentle, tender, and she steeled her heart, pushing away the pinpricks of want and desire trying to find a way in.

Unable to see, panic grew in her stomach, like a seedling eager for light. She inhaled, the sound harsh through her clenched teeth.

"Is it too tight?" The deep rumble of his voice reverberated in the space between them, causing goosebumps to form on her arms.

"It...it's fine." Still bound by the magical rope, she couldn't hide her trembling fingers, so she fisted them. "I don't suppose you'll give me a hint as to where we're headed."

"You'll see once we get there. Well, I guess you won't *see*," he chuckled, the sound one she was getting used to and liking a bit more than she should.

He trailed his fingers down her arm until he slid his palm against hers, clasping her hand. The sensual nature of his touch lit up her skin, and she wanted more. With a quick tug, he drew her forward, beyond her cage and into the hallway.

Her vision gone, her other senses heightened, and she used her natural bear instincts to the fullest. She inhaled, and his scent of pepper and lime, along with the ancient stone and metallic tang of the bars, filtered into her nose. His booted feet scraping against the stone floor, along with hers, resonated down the corridor.

After only a few steps, he stopped. She plowed into him, her body molding to his backside. Strength and power rippled over the muscles in his back, and she had the sudden desire to run her hands over his broad shoulders, feel the warmth of his skin beneath her fingertips.

"Ginnia..."

"Don't worry, Saar. You'll make it out before they come." The female's words were like a premonition, and a chill settled over Kaelyn's nerves.

"Be good, Muzzie." He didn't linger, but tugged Kaelyn along, his pace rushed.

A restlessness built in her chest. "Where are we going? Are we leaving the Keep?"

"It's best if you don't know."

She stopped in her tracks, digging in her heels. "Tell me."

An exasperated breath eased from him. He tugged her forward, more encouragement then force. "Come. We don't have time for this."

She pursed her lips. "I won't cooperate until you do."

71

A low growl burst from him. This time, his tug left no doubt about who was in charge here.

She slammed into him. Her breasts crushed against his chest.

Saar wrapped his arm around her waist, holding her in place.

The stubble on his chin scraped against her cheek, sending a wave of delight over her skin. His lips brushed along her neck until they teased the sensitive skin at her ear. "If you don't come with me, you'll die here, right now. Is that what you want?"

She shivered in his embrace because of her need and want of this male and because of his shocking words. "N...no."

"Then let's go." He released her as quickly as he'd drawn her to him.

Confusion, need, and anger burned inside, fueling her inner bear. She gnashed her teeth. The warning clack echoed against the walls.

"Don't!" His word was a command and that sparked her desire to fight him all the more.

Saar yanked her to him, wrapping his arms around her once again.

Her hands landed on his firm, muscular chest. She pressed into him, her body molding to his. A tingle of excitement travelled between them, and a part of her wanted to nip him for his insolence. "Are you going to kiss me again?"

He cradled her head is his palm as if he had every right. "Do you want me to?"

"No... Yes."

Before she could take another breath, his lips met hers, devouring her with a possessive, demanding kiss.

She mewled under his onslaught and curled her fingers around his shirt, keeping him there. He deepened the kiss, and her inner bear stirred at his possessiveness, his requirement she comply.

Desire and need warred with her independence, her desire to battle him. Confusion reigned.

His insistent kisses softened, becoming gentler. What this male could do to her given the chance.

He broke the kiss, but still cradled her head in his palms. Their heavy panting reverberated off the stone walls. She hated her reaction, her blatant yearning for him.

"Quit fighting me." His soft breath teased her cheek, and she cursed the blindfold. If only she could read his expression.

"Keep your friends close and your enemies closer." Theron's words flitted through her mind.

She exhaled, her shoulders loosening the tension she hadn't realized she'd held. "Fine."

He released his hold on her. "We should be outside soon. Then I'll remove your blindfold." He caressed her fingers. As he closed his grip around her hand, she didn't resist.

He continued down his chosen path. They turned a corner, then another. Before long, she was lost. Their boots slapping the stone floor and their labored breaths were the only sounds.

She couldn't take the silence any longer. Besides, maybe she could get some intel out of him. "Tell me something. What is it like for you, here in the Keep?"

He flinched, but didn't slow. "Why do you ask?"

"I'm curious. From what little I've seen, the Keep seems like a remarkable place."

A sudden rush of heat warmed the air, the source coming from the walls.

"I've lived within the Keep's protected walls for more than five hundred years. It is our safe haven. We live normal lives, as much as can be expected given the war."

"I can't even imagine." As nomads, her kind hadn't lived in one place for more than a couple of years. "What do you do here when you're not fighting, when you have free time?"

He slowed, and the material of his jacket creaked as he turned. "If we're going to play this game, I'd say it's your turn. Tell me, what do you do with your 'free time.'" The warmth of his breath teased her cheek.

Cognizant of his closeness, she inhaled. His essence eased into her lungs, filling her with his delicious masculine scent. Heat radiated from her chest to her cheeks. "Um…"

He chuckled. "That's what I thought. Be careful what kind of games you play, little bear." Before she could respond, he tugged her forward once again.

A flash of anger flitted along her veins. "Don't call me that. I'm not little."

"You are to me." His rough, gravelly voice draped around her.

Awareness of just how large a male he was heated her cheeks. "I'm not playing you, if that's what you think. I just want to...I...I can't stand the silence."

"Then you do the talking. Tell me whatever you'd like. Perhaps something you enjoy."

Suddenly tongue-tied, she couldn't speak. "I...I... When I have time, I love to roll in the ferns. In my bear form."

He squeezed her hand. "Feisty as you are, I'll bet you do. What else?"

She exhaled. "I enjoy campfires, stories, and good company with my friends and fam..." The familiar weight of her whistle against her chest caused a lump to form in the back of her throat. "I...carve wood."

He stilled, and she bumped into him. With a gentleness she was fast becoming used to, he gripped her arm to steady her. His fingers grazed along her neck following her chain to her bear's head whistle.

"Did you make this?" His voice was low, reverent.

"Yes." Her tongue seemed to expand in her mouth, preventing her from saying anything more.

"Then we have something in common. Although I've never done anything as elaborate as this," his fingers brushed her collar bone as he traced the outline of her whistle, "I whittle."

She swallowed. "What do you make?"

A soft breath eased from him. "Toothpicks. They provide a measure of peace, both in the creation and in the use."

"I understand." This male was more than just her enemy, he was real. He had a life of his own here at the Keep. A question burned in her mind. She had to know. "Do you have a family?"

He withdrew his hand, and the sudden lack of his warmth left a cold spot over her heart. Dread filled its place. "Not anymore. My parents and my brother died long ago. Come, we continue."

She stumbled to keep up with his pace. He never mentioned a mate. Frustration twisted into a knot in her gut. She shouldn't care one way or the other, but she did. "Do you have a female?"

Swift as a cat, he turned and pinned her against the wall. Her bound hands flattened against his chest, trapped in the space between them. His warm breath cascaded down her throat, sending a thrill of desire straight to her core.

"What are you doing?" She pushed against him, into the hard planes of his chest.

"Perhaps your blindfold has made you forget." He eased back enough to grip her wrists with one of his large palms. After seizing her fingers, he planted them on the scar at his cheek. "Do you think a female would want me, want this?"

She resisted the urge to pull away. No doubt he expected her to be disgusted by his disfigurement. Tentatively, she stroked her fingers over the scar. "It's so smooth. How did you—"

A groan of pure anguish eased from his lips, and he pushed away from the wall, away from her. "*Craya!* No more questions."

The tremor started in her knees then travelled up her torso and down her arms, leaving goosebumps in its wake. Her chest ached for this strong, proud warrior who hid his pain behind his rough exterior. He'd unsettled her far more than she cared to admit.

Saar exhaled, long and slow. "I'm sorry. Come, we're almost there."

He slid his hand over hers and they continued on their path.

"Tell me one more thing. Ginnia mentioned you don't shift, that it's forbidden and no one has been able to transform back. Is that true?"

"Not entirely. We used to shift, before the great scourge occurred over five hundred years ago, wiping out over half of our kind. Ever since then, we haven't been able to shift and return to human form. Not until..." He exhaled in a loud rush.

"Please, share with me."

He remained silent for a long stretch. "Two of our males recently bonded to human females. Their mates were able to help them return from their beast forms. No one is certain why."

He didn't elaborate, and she didn't want to press him any further.

An owl's hoot, faint and distant, filtered through the tunnel.

"Is it dark outside?" She'd lost track of time and didn't know if it was day or night.

"Yes, the moon is full. There are still several hours until dawn. Be careful of the blackberry vines."

"Blackberry vines?"

A thorn's sharp tip scraped along her arm. The scent of her blood filled the air. Another branch caught a strand of her hair, ripping it from her scalp. That was it, not her hair. She pushed at the vines, trying to keep them from her.

"Here, let me help you." The branches gave way, and Saar tugged her from the brambles. His thumb rubbed the spot on her arm. "You don't look too worse for wear."

She reached for the blindfold, eager to remove the material.

He gripped her hands, stopping her. "Not yet. We need to go a bit farther. You can't know the location of this entrance."

"Once you let go, nothing can stop me from removing the blindfold."

"I know," he said softly, "but I'm asking you to wait."

Her breath caught in her throat.

He let her go.

The pads of her fingers twitched in her eagerness to remove the offending cloth. Yet, she didn't. Heat raced up her throat and into her cheeks. She'd willingly complied with his request. That was something she rarely did and only with a select few. Her heart skipped a beat.

Perhaps the little seer, Ginnia, was right. Maybe he was her mate. *No...not possible.*

He gripped her hand once again and stepped away. She followed, but the next time they stopped, all bets were off.

CHAPTER 15

*S*aar circled through the forest, crossing his tracks time and again. His boots scraped against the bits of stone and rough dirt at his feet. Kicked up by the tip of his shoe, a pebble skittered across his path. Jerking this way and that, the bouncing rock was an eerie symbol for his erratic emotions.

He yanked a toothpick from his pocket and shoved it between his lips. Twirling the end with his tongue, he forced his mind from the female behind him. Kaelyn sent his pulse into the ether and scrambled his brain.

Soon, he'd have to kill her. A tremor rippled through him followed by a sheen of sweat on his skin. His marking for courage and the one for loyalty burned on the back of his shoulder.

"Are we there yet?" Kaelyn's sweet voice drew him from his musing, grounding him.

He stopped. No point in delaying. Each moment he stalled picked away at his resolve. "We've covered our tracks several times. You won't be able to trace back to the entrance from here."

Not that it would matter since she'd be dead soon. Ice froze in his veins at the thought.

She raised her hands, her wrists still bound by the magical rope, and she reached for the blindfold.

He gripped her hands, stopping her.

She inhaled, and sweet goddess, when her mouth parted, it was all he could do not to kiss those full, plump lips.

A groan of pure frustration eased from him, turning into a growl. "Allow me."

"If you insist." Relaxing her fingers, she let go of the material.

"I do." With a tenderness she brought out in him, he untied the knot at the back of her head. The material slid over her nose and cheeks. As he pulled his hands away, he toyed with her dark strands. The silky tresses teased his skin, sending pinpricks of desire along his fingers.

He handed her the golden cloth, and she shoved it into her pocket. As her gaze rose to meet his, her eyebrows drew together over her mesmerizing hazel-green eyes.

Obey your king. Kill her.

Now...or never.

Sweat beaded his forehead. A drop slid down the bridge of his nose and dripped off the end.

Kaelyn took a step back. "What are you—"

Focusing his attention on her, he drew his sword from his scabbard. Blade scraping against metal echoed through the trees.

Her beautiful eyes widened, and she captured him in her snare.

His inner beast screamed.

Mind racing, the compulsion to protect Kaelyn warred with his commitment to please his king. A snarl ripped from his throat, low and menacing. The beast became dangerously close to taking control and raised the hair on his arms.

"No...no...no...No...NO...NO!" He hurled his sword at a nearby tree. The blade embedded into the thick bark with a loud thunk.

Blood pounded at his temple. Saar's vision swam.

He couldn't kill Kaelyn, not now, maybe not ever.

Noeh...I failed you.

His marking for loyalty burned hotter than it ever had before.

Although he couldn't see it, he knew without a doubt, the dark line faded. Self-loathing soured his stomach, sending bile up his throat. He wanted to despise Kaelyn, hate her for what she did to him, but he didn't. Instead, relief that she lived flooded through him, washing away any common sense along with it.

Silence filled the forest broken only by their combined, stilted breaths.

A visible shiver wracked her body, but she held her ground. "W... Why didn't you kill me?"

"I couldn't." A short laugh slipped from his lips.

Her brow furrowed. She slid her finger over his arm, tingling his skin. "You're shaking. Are you all right?"

Her concern for him broke through his confusion, along with the repercussions of what he'd done. He couldn't breathe.

Traitor...

Saar's knee buckled, bringing him down. His kneecap hit a rock. A shooting pain ran up his thigh. He deserved that and a whole lot more.

Kaelyn knelt next to him. "What can I do?"

He peered at her.

Her keen eyes bore into him, searching deep into his soul as if she understood him on a primal level. Strength, determination, and tenderness reflected in their mesmerizing depths. The silver rope wrapped around her wrists shimmered in the moonlight. A lump formed in his throat.

Without a doubt, he knew what he had to do. He stood, forcing his injured knee to cooperate. It protested by sending another round of pain up his leg. He touched the rope. "Let me remove this for you."

"...but you're injured. I want to help." Her tender words only stoked the fire of his resolve.

He untied the bindings, and the rope slipped to the hard-packed Earth at their feet. "You can't help me."

"Why not?" She parted her full, plump lips as if begging for another kiss.

A tic started in his jaw, spurned by his determination. "Because we're enemies, aren't we?"

She blinked. A shadow crossed her face, but she took a step back.

He smiled, and the familiar tugging of his skin reminded him of the other reason they could never be together. "It's time for you to go. You're free. Run, little bear. Run."

Before he could react, she kissed him, hard, then fled into the forest.

CHAPTER 16

*G*aetan held the tray with one hand, with the other, he gripped his cane. His boot scraped across the stone floor, his gait uneven thanks to the constant ache in his malformed leg. One step after another, he proceeded down the corridor. His destination, the stronghold to visit his sister.

Ginnia, Ginnia, Ginnia. Why on this planet did she let Mauree out of her cell? No matter how many times he'd asked her, she'd never revealed why she'd let Mauree escape.

He shook his head. As the eldest Stiyaha in the Keep, he'd learned long ago to trust Ginnia's visions. She'd said Mauree couldn't die—as in *shouldn't die.* He'd never known Ginnia to be wrong before, and he prayed this time wouldn't be her first mistake.

"Gaetan! You've come to visit!" Ginnia leaned against the cell's bars. A few strands of her hair poked through, as if eager to escape.

He chuckled at her enthusiasm, his chest lightening. "Yes, Angel, I'm here. I brought you something."

"Ooh," she inhaled, "I smell soup!" Her soft claps echoed from her cell.

He placed the tray at the edge of her door and passed the brew to her through the bars. Her eyes gleamed with appreciation. She took the bowl from him, and as she sat on her bed, the blue and green comforter bunched under her knees.

Eerie silence from the adjacent cell caused the hair at his nape to rise. He twisted around. An unnatural coldness hit him full force. The cell was empty, the open lock on the ground.

"Ginnia," he whipped his head to look at her, "where is the prisoner, Kaelyn?"

She pulled the spoon from her mouth and licked her lips. "Gone."

"Angel, you can do better than that." He lowered his voice.

Ginnia tugged the bowl against her chest and turned her back to him.

A headache throbbed behind his eyes. Gaetan loved his sister, but there were times she was as much of a pain as his deformed leg. After what he'd done, though, she'd deserved nothing but his love and patience. He approached the cell and wrapped his hand around one of the bars. "It's okay, Angel. Come here. Let me give you a hug."

She ran to him, and he wrapped her in his embrace as best he could, the bars cold and hard between them.

"I miss you," she whispered tenderly.

A lump formed in his throat. "I miss you, too, Angel."

He held her for several long moments until she relaxed against him. He pulled back, tucked a few stray strands of hair behind her ear, and peered at her. "Now, Ginnia, tell me what happened."

Her eyes tracked back and forth as she studied him. "Please don't be mad at Saar."

"Saar had something to do with this? Did he transport the prisoner somewhere?"

She tilted her head and stared at the ceiling. "Well, you could say that."

"Where did he take her?"

She pointed down the corridor, the opposite direction from which Gaetan had come. The stronghold was the last outpost before the corridors wound into a maze.

"Did he say why he went that way?"

She scrunched her eyebrows together and stepped away. "Yes, but I don't want to tell."

"It's okay, Angel. No one is going to hurt you." *Not as long as I'm alive.*

She crossed her arms. "I'm not worried about me. I'm worried about Saar."

"Okay, why?"

"He said something you won't like."

"What did he say?" Dread toyed with Gaetan's nerves, scraping its claws over him again and again.

Her pale gray eyes rimmed with tears. "Promise me you won't hurt him."

"I couldn't hurt a fly."

Her features brightened, the child inside happy once again. "He said to Kaelyn, 'I'm taking you for a little walk, blindfolded.' "

White spots formed in Gaetan's vision. Blood pounded in his ears. He couldn't process her words, unable to fathom what had happened here. "Are...are you telling me Saar left with the prisoner?"

She nodded, but her lip trembled.

"It's okay, Angel. Thank you for telling me." He reached through the bars, encouraging her forward.

She came to him again, and he wrapped his hand around hers, giving her a gentle squeeze. "What else do you know?"

A mischievous grin tugged at her lip. "I can get out if I want to."

His lungs expanded. She was so proud of her abilities, he didn't have the heart to bring her down. "Yes, but you won't."

She raised her eyebrows, surprise registering in her eyes. "Why not?"

He chuckled. "Because I'm asking you not to. Stay here. Do as Noeh asks."

She pursed her lips, but there was child-like mirth in her eyes. "Okay. I do it for you and for him."

He squeezed her hand again. "Good job, Angel."

A heavy weight settled onto his shoulders. His next stop—the throne room. He had to tell Noeh his Commander of Arms and the prisoner were gone.

CHAPTER 17

$\mathcal{W}$ith careful, measured steps, Saar approached the large cedar. He placed his hand against the rough bark and peered over a low branch. Through the dense forest, the solitary bear lumbered over the rough terrain with ease. Its black coat appeared almost a deep shade of blue as the sleek fur shimmered in the moonlight.

Even in her altered form, Kaelyn was beautiful.

As she crested over the hill, he continued his pursuit, keeping downwind and out of earshot. The last thing he wanted was for her to know he followed her. He told himself he did this to gather more evidence about his enemy, maybe find out the location of Mauree's hideout, but in truth, he didn't want to let Kaelyn go.

And he couldn't return to the Keep. Only death awaited him there.

Saar's stomach hardened, and his marking for loyalty, courage, and honor all burned, hot and fevered, on the back of his shoulder. He reached beneath his shirt and rubbed the spot, but couldn't wipe away the truth.

"Father was right, I'm selfish and now, I'm a traitor." The words beat into his soul, shredding him from the inside out. Maybe if he found Mauree's hideout, brought that bit of intel back with him, the sting of his death would lessen. Yet, providing Noeh with the information would bring death to Kaelyn's door.

His chest tightened, squeezing the breath from his lungs.

Neither choice was optimal.

No, there was no going back, not after his treasonous act. Perhaps he'd become a lone fighter in the war, similar to some of the rogue Panthera warriors, the ones that roamed the edges of the Keep's territory.

Only he'd have to avoid his own kind. Chances were they'd send a search party for him as soon as they discovered he was gone. He couldn't allow them to find him. How strange...he'd gone from trusted warrior to traitor in a matter of moments and all for a beautiful female he could never be with. Irony was such a bitch.

He tugged a toothpick from his pocket, his last one, and jabbed it between his lips. The familiar stick calmed his ragged nerves, soothing him, and he refocused his attention on Kaelyn's retreating form. He placed his palm on the hilt of his sword. At the moment, his trusty weapon was his only friend.

Kaelyn came to a small clearing. She morphed into her human form, her tight-fitting pants and shirt reformed onto her luscious curves. Long and full, her hair fluttered in the breeze, as if waving to him, saying their last goodbyes.

A tightness in his chest caused his breath to hitch. Unwilling to let her go just yet he shortened the distance between them, eager to remain close.

She drew her yellow braiding cloth from her pocket and studied the material. Her gaze rose skyward, and a pained expression strained her features. With a delicate caress, she parted her hair into two sections and using the cloth as the third twine, she braided the long tresses.

Mesmerized, his fingertips twitched. The urge to touch her luxurious mane, and feel the silky smoothness for himself, wafted over him. He curled his hand into a fist.

A loud whistle pierced the air, a tune one he'd heard before. He stiffened.

Kaelyn wrapped her fingers around her whistle and brought the bear's head ornament to her lips. A soft melodic trill eased from her, the beautiful melody seeping into him. Part of him wished her call was for him.

A male with dark hair stepped from between the trees. Quick and firm, he tugged her into his embrace, his arms tight around her waist.

"Theron!" She buried her face against his chest.

Spots of anger flashed in Saar's vision, and he bit the toothpick in half. He jerked it out of his mouth and tossed the broken stick onto the soft pine needles at his feet.

His beast pounded against Saar's control, eager to break free, battle the male who dared touch *his* female. He hardened his hold on his inner beast. *She's not mine.* Even as he thought the words, he understood the lie hidden within.

Theron stepped back, a relieved smile on his face. He studied her for a moment then pointed to the empty pouch at her waist.

She shook her head, and her lips moved, but a sudden breeze picked up, carrying away the words.

Theron untied one of the maces at his belt and handed it to her. She hefted the weapon, her bicep flexing under the weight.

Saar's lungs expanded as pride for her filled him. She was a strong, beautiful female, so different from the ones at the Keep. This little Ursus bear went toe to toe with him, and he admired her feistiness and spunk.

Another male, a tad shorter, but with the same bulky build and dark hair, joined the two. He gave Kaelyn a quick bow, as if she were royalty.

A bow? Before Saar could dwell on the trio, the astringent stench of Gossum filled the air.

He tensed and drew his sword. The blade quivered, as eager as he was to battle the creatures.

"Not yet, my friend," he whispered.

Four Gossum, their bald heads gleaming in the light, slipped from the trees. So focused on Kaelyn, he'd relaxed his guard, but their timing was perfect. He needed to let loose his frustration, and they were as good an excuse as any.

The four Gossum lumbered toward him, their tongues snapping from their mouths. They wore dark pants and shirts over their hair-less bodies and blended in with the surroundings. One with a remnant of gray hair on his head outran his comrades. A shriek rose from his throat as he closed the distance.

Saar strengthened his grip on his sword and focused on his enemy. He prepared himself, his inner beast growling. Many times in the past he'd faced multiple foes and survived. He'd do so again tonight.

The first Gossum, Gray Hair, launched himself at Saar, the tips of his sharp nails gleaming in the light.

Saar swung his sword.

Screeeee.

His weapon sliced through the Gossum's throat. The severed head landed on the ferns with a splat. Momentum knocked the body off balance, and the creature stiffened, then slid to the ground in a pile of black inky goo.

Saar didn't have time to celebrate the quick victory. The other three Gossum were on him in a moment. He parried, blocking the barbed tip of a tongue with his arm band. Sharp claws tore through his pants and into the muscles in his thigh. The scent of his blood filled the air.

With his free hand, he gripped the creature around the throat and squeezed. Its breath rattled in its throat.

The remaining Gossum stung him on the leg, the shoulder, the knee.

He released the dead creature and swung his sword, again and again, severing hands, shredding flesh, slicing through bones. A howl tore from his throat fueled by his inner beast and his rage. When all was said and done, all that remained of his enemy was the dark black sludge coating the ferns and small plants at his feet.

His breath heaved in and out of his lungs. Pain rippled up his leg, his arm, his shoulder thanks to the Gossum's muscle-numbing venomous tongues and sharp claws.

The rustle of feet trampling underbrush halted him. He turned toward the sound.

Two Ursus males sped toward him.

One male morphed into a bear, his silver coat reflecting the few rays of moonlight that filtered through the trees.

The other male, this *Theron*, the one who had held Kaelyn so tenderly, had eyes that gleamed with murderous intent. He gripped a mace in his hand, fingers clenched around the wooden handle.

Saar set his feet and raised his sword. Multiple Gossum, no problem. Multiple Ursus? Good question.

They appeared more formidable than their weaker counterparts, but he had no doubt he'd prevail.

Where was Kaelyn? Was she safe? The errant thought ripped through his mind, but he didn't have time to dwell on it.

Theron was the first to arrive. He twirled the spiked ball above his head. The air hummed, louder and louder, with each repetition. With a quick flick, he brought the mace down. Saar blocked the blow with his sword. The clank of metal against metal echoed between the trees.

Saar's muscles shook from the vibration, his fingers numbing from the impact. Through sheer force of will, he maintained his grip. He swung the sword, catching the chain that attached the ball to the handle around the sword's tip. He yanked the weapon from his enemy. With a loud thunk, the mace landed amid the ferns.

The bear displayed its fangs, a loud growl rumbling from its chest. Before Saar could recover, the creature swiped its paws down his back. The excruciating pain fueled his inner beast. He kicked out, slamming the bear in the snout. The creature roared and kept its distance.

Theron retrieved his mace. He swung it above his head. The mighty weapon reverberated, undulating the air in waves.

Saar caught movement to his right and dared a quick glance.

Kaelyn ran toward him, mace raised. Her hair trailed behind her, bobbing with each step. Strength and determination flowed from her. She was beautiful. Pain and regret etched lines around her eyes.

Once, he'd been an honorable, trusted warrior. Now, he was

nothing but a traitor. To die at the hands of his enemy was what he deserved.

The bear swiped his clawed paw over Saar's chest. Pain bloomed, sending white sparks through his vision. A roar of anguish burst from him. Theron's mace slammed into his wrist. He lost his grip. His trusted weapon slid to the ground.

Screeee.

A whoosh of air caressed his cheek, a precursor of...

Kaelyn's mace connected with his temple.

Darkness claimed him.

$\sim$

Kaelyn's breath heaved in and out of her mouth. Ever relentless and powerful, the urge to fight, battle, and kill Saar burned in her veins, fueled by her connection to Zedron. She'd held back from delivering a killing blow, and the pain still rippled up her arm and into her mind.

The familiar hum of Theron's mace whipping through the air yanked Kaelyn from her tormented thoughts. His muscles bunched under his shirt with the mace's last revolution.

The mace swung toward Saar's chest.

Kaelyn launched herself at Theron, knocking his aim off balance. They tumbled to the ground. The ball's pointed tips embedded into a nearby stump.

A low chuff and the distinct sound of running paws drew closer. The other Ursus warrior, Jacinth, barreled toward them in bear form. His claws dug into the soft loam, flicking dirt into the air with each step.

No! She scrambled to her feet and straddled Saar's supine form. "Do not kill this male. I forbid it."

Jacinth lumbered to the side, his claws narrowly missing Saar's chest.

Kaelyn's pulse pounded at her temple, her quick breaths providing the oxygen her muscles demanded.

"What's going on, Kaelyn?" Theron rose to his feet.

Jacinth transformed into his human form, clothes reforming onto his body. His gaze narrowed on her.

Kaelyn ignored them both and knelt next to Saar who lay on the soft ferns at the edge of the path.

Unconscious, the long lashes that graced his cheek made him seem angelic even with the scar that cut across his face. Blood coated his arm, his leg, his forehead.

She'd hurt him. Self-hatred and loathing roiled in her stomach.

Theron stepped forward, his brow creased. "Why shouldn't we kill him? He's a Stiyaha, our enemy."

She raised her chin. "Mauree is looking for a way into the Keep. He," she pointed to Saar, "brought me through a manual entrance."

Jacinth scoffed. "Lead us there."

She stood, and a low, threatening growl curled in her chest. "I don't know its location. He blindfolded me and circled our tracks too many times. Looking for a way in is pointless."

Jacinth leaned forward. "What do you plan to do?"

Indecision had torn at her as she'd watched Saar fight. She'd admired his skill, his strength, and his determination. He'd dispatched the four Gossum with ease. A mixture of admiration and regret coiled together inside. She forced a smile. "Interrogate him."

"What?"

Theron rested his hand on Jacinth's shoulder. "Stand down, warrior. Don't forget you address our queen. Kaelyn is right."

Theron peered at her, then glanced at Saar. "This male has information Mauree covets. We would be wise to return him to the lake house."

The tic in Theron's jaw and his stiff posture indicated they weren't done with this conversation, but at least he didn't interrogate her here, in front of Jacinth.

Jacinth bowed low. "Forgive me, Kaelyn. I forget my manners."

She raised her hand. "Help Theron carry Saar to Mauree. With the knock to the head and the amount of venom he took, I doubt he'll wake anytime soon." She wanted to rush to his side, attend to his injuries herself, free him, but she couldn't let the others know how much he'd affected her.

Brows drawn low, her gaze tracked over Saar's motionless form. She couldn't care for him the way her heart wanted. *He's the enemy.*

Ginnia's soft, child-like laughter echoed between her ears.

CHAPTER 18

*A*lora tucked the bedspread over her pillow and straightened the end to align with the bed's wooden frame. The cloth wasn't quite perfect, so she tugged on it until the material's edge met her approval.

She peered out the window. Through a natural hole in the Rolmdew tree, a deep purple glowed in the distance, foreshadowing the rise of Lemuria's only sun.

Veromé would be here any moment.

Her chest lightened, and she twirled the gold bracelet around her wrist, the one he'd given to her as an anniversary gift.

The familiar scent of oceans, salty and fresh, wafted by on the breeze. *Veromé.*

Eager to see her mate, she turned around. He materialized in the center of the room, bit by bit, the pieces forming right before her eyes. He'd returned from his dark place, the one he went to during the night. How she cherished the brief moments at sunrise and sunset, their only time together.

His smile, the one she'd fallen for, tugged at his lips. He opened his arms in invitation, and she raced into his embrace. As he held her close to his chest, she breathed in his scent, committing the salty, fresh fragrance to memory so she could make it through another day without him.

"It is always good to have you in my arms." His deep, strong, masculine voice rumbled in his chest.

She relished his embrace, holding on, not wanting to ever let him go. "I have so much to tell you."

He pulled back just enough to study her. His brow furrowed over his beautiful blue eyes. "What is it? Is something wrong?"

She ran her finger along his jawline, enjoying how the stubble teased her skin. "No, nothing is wrong. Quite the contrary, in fact."

Worry lines formed around his eyes. "I don't like the sound of that. What are you up to?"

Feigning irritation, she pursed her lips. "Why do you always assume I'm up to something?"

Cradling her face in his palm, he tracked his thumb over her bottom lip. "Past experience is a good indication of future behavior."

She pouted then ran her tongue over his thumb, enticing him.

"You tease me," he hissed before claiming her with a deep, sensual kiss.

She leaned into him, her body quivering beneath his caress. Between their thin clothing, her hardened nipples pressed against his chest.

He groaned, the vibration traveling through their connection from his lips into hers. Long and hard, his erection twitched along her abdomen.

Good. She enjoyed teasing him, but missed him just as much.

He broke the kiss and placed his forehead against hers. "Tell me. What happened?"

She focused on his beautiful eyes. "Carine came to visit me tonight."

His brow furrowed. "Zedron's slave? Why?"

"We met in the market and I invited her over. I didn't think she'd take me up on my offer, but I'm glad she did." She couldn't contain her smile as it bloomed over her face. "I think she hates him as much as I do."

Veromé's gaze narrowed. "Why don't I like the sound of this?"

"Come, let me show you something." She drew away from him, gripped his hand, and stepped to her dresser.

She picked up the small disc sitting on the worn wood and held it between her fingers, smiling slyly at him. The deep blue shimmered in the light.

Her chest swelled, and she couldn't help but tease him. "Do you know what this is?"

He crossed his arms, but his lip curled at the corner into a delightful grin. "A visus bacin recording device. Did you put something on there just for me?"

She choked out a laugh then straightened her shoulders. "No, it's not mine. Carine brought it to me. It belongs to Zedron."

"What?" Veromé's features slackened.

She held up the disc for his inspection. "This little thing will help me win the war." With a quick flick, she palmed the sphere and shook her fist. "I've got you Zedron, you cheater."

Veromé inhaled. "What did he do?"

She glanced out the window. The sky was as bright as she'd seen it in a long time. Soon, the familiar tug on her insides would start. She had to hurry.

"Do you remember Ram? Aramie and Demir killed him. Seems that pissed Zedron off. He prevented Ram from returning to Lemuria after he died and threw him in a broken human body. That's against the rules and I have the proof," she held up the disc, "in here."

"What did the council say? Did they sanction him?"

She shrugged, trying to look as nonchalant as possible.

Veromé tsked. "Don't tell me you didn't show them the recording device."

She raised her chin. "I haven't decided yet how I want to use this information."

He inhaled. "You're going to see him, Zedron, aren't you?"

"So what if I am?"

Alora…" He shook his head, his handsome features tightening.

The familiar tug started in her gut. For once, she was glad to go. As she faded into her dark place for the day, Veromé's last words echoed in her mind. *Don't take matters into your own hands.*

CHAPTER 19

Gaetan rested his palm against the door to the royal family's private bedchamber. Cool and rough, the ancient wood was one he hadn't touched in years. Only something dire would bring him to seek out Noeh in the one place his king could find a moment's respite from the war.

The muscles in his leg cramped. Triggered by the spasm, a jolt of pain travelled up his thigh and into his hip. He held his breath, letting the agony wash over him. White spots formed in his vision and his mouth went dry.

Out of habit, he reached into the small satchel at his waist and popped one of the pain relieving pills into his mouth. The bitter tang eased the tension, his brain recognizing the upcoming relief before it even flowed into his bloodstream. In the back of his mind, he understood he walked a fine line, but he couldn't stop himself.

With the pain under control, he rapped his knuckles against the wood. The sound echoed down the hall. One of the sunstones lining the Keep's walls flared to life then subsided.

Muffled voices, soft and unintelligible, filtered through the cracks in the doorframe.

"One moment," Noeh's deep voice resonated from behind the door.

Heavy footsteps approached. The door swung open, causing a breeze to rush over Gaetan's shoulders, almost dragging him inside.

He glanced at his king.

Noeh wore a hand-tailored buttoned-down shirt tucked into his waistband. Around his large frame, Gaetan spotted a small table with a place setting for two and a covered tray. The scent of freshly baked bread and roast beef filled the room.

Gaetan cleared his throat. "I don't want to disturb you before your meal."

Noeh narrowed his gaze, concern etched in his furrowed brow. "Nonsense. You are welcome here, always. Come in, please."

With effort, Gaetan forced his battered leg to move. His knee creaked, more a feeling than an actual sound. He eyed the old, familiar place.

The large antique bed with the carved wooden footboard sat against the back wall. Above the bed hung the picture of Noeh as a youth, playing a game of stones with his mother and father.

A twinge cut through Gaetan's chest. The painting was a remembrance of a happier time.

"Would you like to sit down, old friend?" Noeh motioned to the antique desk situated in the corner. With tree trunks for legs, the massive furniture took up more than its fair share of space. Even from this distance, the sunstones embedded in the wooden top reflected the light from the gems lining the walls. Placed by its side, the familiar well-worn wooden chair beckoned him.

Gaetan sighed, and with his cane leading the way, he headed for his relief. "Thank you."

Noeh gripped the edge of the wooden footboard, his ever-knowing eyes assessing him. The slight clink of his ring as he tapped it against the wood was in counterpoint to Gaetan's cane on the stone floor.

Gaetan settled himself on the chair, leaned his cane against the desk, and rubbed his knee.

Noeh's attention flicked to Gaetan's leg then met his eyes. "Something's wrong. Tell me."

Gaetan pinched the bridge of his nose. *Where to begin?* "I bring news you don't wish to hear."

Noeh's boots scraped against the stone floor. He placed his warm palm on Gaetan's shoulder. "Are you ill? I will do anything in my power to help you."

Gaetan lowered his hand and peered at his king and good friend, the one he'd raised ever since Noeh's parents died during the great scourge. Worry lines rimmed Noeh's eyes, and his features were drawn, as if he expected bad news. Gaetan exhaled. "I'm fine. It's not me you should concern yourself with."

Noeh wiped his palm over his face. "Thank the gods. Then who?"

The door to Noeh's antechamber creaked open. Melissa stood in the doorway, dressed in a beautiful silk dress. She smiled. "Gaetan, I'm glad to see you."

He bowed his head then raised it again so Noeh could read his lips. "Forgive me, my queen, for intruding, but I'm glad I caught you both."

Noeh strode toward his mate and wrapped his arm around her shoulder. "Gaetan, please continue."

A slight chill lifted the hairs on the back of his neck, and he rubbed the skin, trying to relieve the tension growing there. "I don't know how to tell you this other than to just say it. Saar removed the prisoner from her cell and left the Keep."

The muscles in Noeh's shoulders stiffened. "What?"

Noeh glanced at Melissa. They stared at each other for a moment, having a private conversation. Ever since Melissa died and Noeh brought her back to life, they shared a soul. As such, they communicated telepathically.

Gaetan and Saar were the only ones aware of their special bond.

Melissa placed her hand on Noeh's arm. His jaw flexed, and he returned his attention to Gaetan. "How do you know this? Speak slowly."

"I took a cup of Ginnia's favorite soup to her. The prisoner's cell was empty, the lock open, unbroken on the ground—" A burning sensation warmed his toes then ran up his leg, centering in the ache in his knee. He ground his teeth, letting the agony pass before he continued. "Ginnia said Saar freed the female and took her outside."

"No. Not possible." Noeh's face reddened. He released his hold on Melissa and strode toward Gaetan.

The pain and anguish in Noeh's taut features slid into Gaetan. He hated to see his king so tormented. "You know as well as I, Ginnia doesn't lie."

Noeh slammed his fist onto the wooden desk. Pencils and pens skittered across the surface. One quill rolled over the edge and bounced against the stone floor. "Then you do."

Gaetan's pulse pounded, sending a wave of adrenaline through his body. The flush through his veins eased the pain in his leg, but the tradeoff wasn't worth it. Noeh's sharp words injured him far worse. His breath stalled in his lungs.

Melissa ran her hand over Noeh's shoulder and down his massive bicep. She tugged on his arm. "That's enough."

"*Craya!*" He ran his fingers through his hair. With a loud exhale, he spoke. "Forgive me, my friend. I just can't accept…"

Gaetan sighed. "Neither can I, but the evidence was irrefutable. He took the Ursus female through the tunnels."

Noeh stiffened. "How long ago?"

Gaetan closed his eyes. "Now I need to ask your forgiveness. This happened a few hours ago. I was detained."

Noeh's eyes narrowed. "Detained?"

He nodded. Delayed by an addiction he was loath to admit even to himself.

Noeh closed his eyes.

A ripple ran over Gaetan's nerves, like a dark cloud. The familiar sensation was one he recognized. *Sunrise.*

Noeh opened his eyes and pulled away from Melissa. He approached Gaetan, fisting his hand at his side. "The warriors will search the Keep today. If we don't find them in the tunnels, the pursuit will expand come nightfall. We will find him. Find them both."

Saar was long gone, of that, Gaetan had little doubt. The

Commander of Arms was their best warrior and understood the idio-syncrasies of the Keep's tunnels better than anyone. *Good luck, my friend.* To which he referred, Noeh or Saar, he wasn't quite sure.

Noeh gripped Gaetan's arm. His features had an intensity Gaetan hadn't seen before. "You were my mentor, my father's best friend, and the one Stiyaha I can count on above all others. If anything ever happens to me," his eyes flickered with amber, "I want you to raise Anlon. Raise him as you did me until he's ready to rule. Will you do that for me, my friend?"

Gaetan swallowed. There was no way he could refuse. "I pray it won't come to that, but of course. I'd do anything for you, for him. I vow it." As he said the words, his commitment wrapped around his soul, adding another link to the chain of responsibility already hanging there.

CHAPTER 20

Kaelyn paced outside the small cottage, one of the many that graced the lake house property. Her boots wore a path in the short grass, and when she reached the end of the tiny house, she turned around and retraced her steps.

A nervous energy kept her pace fast, clipped, despite the gnawing tension growing in her gut. With a quick flip of her head, she pitched her braid over her shoulder, the golden silk reminding her of the blindfold and of Saar's gentle touch.

She glanced at the window. The shade was drawn, and the early morning sun's bright glare reflected off the glass. *Saar.* Nausea rose in her throat.

Theron and Jacinth had placed Saar in the small cottage, chaining him to the concrete foundation.

She'd wanted to check on him, ensure that he was all right, but she'd held back. What would they do if they knew the truth? That she'd allowed him to kiss her, had wanted it with a desperation she didn't fully understand.

Her nerves thrummed so hard and fast she thought she'd explode. Instead, she continued on her path, driving one foot in front of the other. The wait would kill her.

A sparrow chirped in a nearby tree, the tiny peep answered by another. What she'd give for such a simple life. Her bear itched to run, let loose some of this energy, but she wouldn't stray too far from Saar.

The slight creak of a door stopped her in her tracks. She jerked toward the noise.

Theron emerged onto the small porch.

Her heart caught in her throat. "Is he—"

Theron raised his hand and shook his head. "He hasn't awoken yet, if that's what you're about to ask."

The tension in her muscles released, like a bucket of water doused on a fire. "H...how bad are his injuries?" She held her breath.

With dark and assessing eyes, he studied her. "He'll live long enough to give us some answers. Don't worry, Jacinth is in there with him. He won't get away."

Unable to maintain his gaze any longer, she peered into the forest. She ran her hand over her face and feigned a tiredness she didn't feel. "Are you on your way to inform Mauree?"

He stepped off the porch's lone stair and approached. When he was within range, he drew her into his embrace. His warm licorice scent worked its way inside, calming her with its familiarity. Family was so important, and the need for revenge boiling in her veins made her clutch him tighter.

She held on for a moment longer then drew away.

Grasping her chin between his thumb and index finger, he gave her a gentle shake. "We should talk first. Walk with me."

Before she could stop him, he started across the lawn, heading for the main house, one tip of its dark roof visible over the tree tops. She ran to catch up with him.

They walked in silence for a moment. Theron cleared his throat. "Now that we're alone, tell me, what happened between you two."

A niggle of fear slipped inside. Irritation rippled right after, chasing the unwanted emotion away. "What do you mean?"

He stopped, his attention focusing on her. "I know you well. You held back. You could've, no, should've killed him, yet you didn't."

"I told you—"

"Don't feed me the 'we could get information from him' line. That wouldn't have stopped the Kaelyn I know from killing an enemy. So, tell me, what happened after he captured you?"

Blazing anger erupted inside. "Strange as it may seem, he was surprisingly nice to me, and then he let me go."

"Smart. I'd have done the same." He continued toward the house.

She gripped his arm, stopping him. "What does that mean?"

"Kaelyn, you're smarter than this. Don't let him fool you. He tracked you searching for the lake house. Had the Gossum not found him when they did, he might've succeeded."

Her heart pounded. *No.* The memory of his touch, his kiss, his soft words all came crashing down on her. Had she really been that naive?

A sheen of sweat broke out on her skin.

He'd taken her for a fool.

She curled her hand into a fist, and the muscles in her arms shook from her rage. "When the time comes, I will be the one to interrogate him."

$\sim$

Mauree leaned on the deck railing and picked at the wood with her fingernail. The warmth of the morning sun crested over the horizon. She rubbed her hands over the terrycloth, enjoying the soft texture against her skin.

Out of the corner of her eye, she spotted Theron trudging through the lawn and heading toward the main house, Kaelyn at his side. *Good.* He'd found his niece and Mauree had her bargaining chip once again.

Warmth flooded her body from her chest down to her feet. Her toes itched, and she wiggled them inside her red pumps. Other than the robe, her shoes were her only bit of clothing covering her at the moment.

Her attention returned to Theron, noting his powerful stride and how his broad shoulders flexed with each step. There was only one thing better than sex...well, no, scratch that. At this point, even winning the war might take a back seat to Theron.

She smiled.

Maybe she could glean a bit of intel from the little kidnapped tramp. Now that, and a quick round with Theron, would make her day. She pushed away from the railing and headed into her room to dress for the occasion.

A few minutes later, she descended the stairs still wearing her favorite red shoes. The short mini and tight knit sweater were the perfect complement to the pumps.

"Well done, if I don't say so myself," she whispered.

Several Gossum hunkered over the massive dining room table, maps spread out before them. Caught up in their own conversation, none seemed to notice her.

She cleared her throat.

The soldiers closest to her turned to look. One male, tall and reed-thin with a patch over one damaged eye, shifted away from the table. He gave her a quick bow. "Do you need something, my lady?"

Mauree's chest expanded at his overt display of respect. "Just keep up the good work."

He deepened his bow, his one eye gleaming from her praise. "As you wish."

After reaching the bottom of the stairs, she stepped onto the polished wooden floor. Her heels clicked with each step, and she had to force herself not to run, not to give in to her eagerness to see Theron.

She entered the kitchen, and the patio door slid open on its track. A breeze blew between the pans hanging over the center island, a soft clank echoing through the room.

Theron stepped inside, Kaelyn close behind.

Kaelyn caught sight of Mauree. Her lip curled.

Mauree's skin crawled, her earlier excitement to see Theron chased away by Kaelyn's attitude. "You're back. How...fitting."

Kaelyn's face reddened, her features a mask of rage.

Theron placed his hand on her shoulder and stepped forward. "We bring news."

"I see you found," she forced a smile and glanced at Kaelyn, "your niece."

Theron pursed his lips, clearly not happy with her response. Well, that was too bad. He'd have a lot more of her attitude to deal with before he was through.

A large bowl filled with oranges, apples, and bananas sat on the expansive kitchen countertop. He wrapped his fingers around a Golden Delicious and offered the fruit to Kaelyn. She shook her head. He shrugged and bit into the crisp rind. Juice sprayed into the air in a fine mist.

"She's not the only one we found," he said between chews.

Mauree's heart stuttered. "What do you mean?"

Theron smiled. "We have a prisoner. Perhaps you know him?"

"What's his name?"

He glanced at Kaelyn.

Still standing in front of the large glass doors, she crossed her arms. "Saar."

Mauree inhaled. Her mind whirred, flashing through possibilities. She tapped her long red fingernail against her lip. "Interesting. Why did you bring him here?"

Kaelyn's mouth thinned, and a zip of adrenaline skipped along Mauree's nerves. How she loved poking at the female bear.

"He brought me through one of the Keep's manual entrances, blindfolded, so I don't know where it is—"

Mauree chuckled. "But he does. Perfect."

This could be good, very good indeed. She glanced through the glass doors. The morning sun brightened the patio, encasing the outdoor furniture in its golden glow. Sticklike and grotesque, the legs from the table and chairs cast long shadows on the cement as if pointing the way. "Where is he?"

"He's in one of the cottages, unconscious. We almost killed him before Kaelyn told us what we had." Theron tossed the apple core into the sink where it bounced against the stainless steel before coming to rest in the garbage disposal's opening.

Mauree raised an eyebrow. "Nice shot. When he wakes, we'll interrogate him."

Kaelyn stepped forward, her chin raised. "I'll do it. I deserve the payback."

Mauree tittered. "We shall see. Why don't you keep tabs on him and let us know when he wakes? In the meantime," she peered at Theron, her gaze raking down his body, "we have some time, don't we?"

CHAPTER 21

*P*ain pounded Saar's skull, pulsing at his temple with each beat of his heart. He inhaled through clenched teeth, and the fragrant scent of sweet peas raced into his lungs. The fog in his brain trapped any rational thoughts from forming, so he concentrated on breathing, letting Kaelyn's unique perfume work into every fiber of his being.

A warm touch, followed by a gentle cool washcloth on his forehead brought him through the gloom.

He opened his eyes.

Blinding light from a bare bulb in the ceiling sent a jab to the back of his eyes, reigniting the pounding in his brain. He tried to sit, but a firm hand on his chest and the rattling of chains stopped him. Metal cuffs bit into his skin.

Confusion, unease, and anger all roiled together in his gut, fighting for dominance.

He lashed out, the tendons in his neck straining from the exertion. "What…"

"Shh…shh… You're okay." Kaelyn's soft words and the warmth of her hands on his bare chest brought him fully alert.

Glancing around, he fought to regain his bearings. He focused on four blank walls, a small table in the corner with an assortment of tools spread across the surface, a broken down chair, and tufts of material sprouting from a hole in the arm. Thick, dark metal clamps bound his wrists and ankles. A heavy chain led to large bolts secured into the concrete floor.

His pulse raced. *Captured.*

Chunks of wood and grit from the hard wooden floor bit into his bare back. Somewhere along the way, they'd removed his shirt. He glanced down. Thank the goddess, they'd allowed him to keep his pants and shoes.

His attention focused on Kaelyn. He raised his hand as far as the chain would allow. With a gentle caress, he stroked the soft, smooth skin on the inside of her arm. "Kaelyn."

A brief flicker of relief passed over her face before her features hardened.

His chest squeezed the breath from him. He hated to see her like that.

"You'll live, for now." She withdrew her hands, and the cold air replaced her warmth.

Memories of the fight in the forest resurfaced in his mind—the Gossum, the bear, Theron, and Kaelyn. Her mace, as if in slow motion, careened toward his head. She'd taken him down. Heaviness settled over his shoulders.

By all accounts, he should be dead. Why didn't she kill him when she'd had the chance? *Because she's my mate...*

Even in his head, the thought was a growl. Was it possible she hadn't wanted him dead? By the thin line of her mouth and her tight features, though, she seemed like she could kill him given the opportunity.

"H...," he cleared his dry throat, "how long have I been here and why am I here?"

"All day. It's early evening now. You're here for information." She stood and turned her back on him, but not before he caught the pained expression in her eyes.

His shoulders ached from the deep scratches, still healing, and his leg tingled, the last of the Gossum's muscle-freezing venom working through his body. He jerked on the chains, testing their strength. They were solid, but they wouldn't hold him. If he were at full power, he could free himself in a matter of moments, but he was still too weak from the attack to try. He'd have to bide his time. "For you, I would sell my soul, but for your friends, no."

She whipped her head around, glaring at him over her shoulder. A flash of anger or, perhaps, desire flitted through her eyes. He wasn't sure which. She turned to face him and crossed her arms. "You'd be wise to—"

The creak of a door echoed from the next room. Heavy footsteps, complemented by a pair of high heels clicking against the wooden floor, grew louder as the new arrivals approached.

Kaelyn's brow furrowed, and she gnawed at her bottom lip. "Please, Saar, do as they ask. Don't—"

The door swung open. A soft breeze filtered into the room. Chokingly sweet, the scent of roses filled the air. *Mauree.*

Rage, bitter and vile, crept up his throat. She added a whole new level to the word 'traitor.'

He yanked on the bindings, and the cuff's sharp edges dug into his skin. The chain pulled taut. A slight creak eased from the bolt, but it didn't give way. He wasn't at full strength, not yet.

Mauree stepped into the room, her arrogance swirling around her like a dark cloud.

The bare skin on his chest prickled as if ants had crawled over him.

Theron, the male he'd battled in the woods, followed her into the room. Behind him came two Gossum, and Saar got a look at their bald heads and dark eyes up close and personal.

The need to battle his enemy sparked anew, and he strained against his bonds.

"Hello, Saar. So good to see you again." Mauree tittered, the high-pitched squeal loud and grating.

Saar curled his lip. "You're a disgrace to all Stiyaha."

She raised an eyebrow. "Have you looked in a mirror lately? Your ugly mug hasn't changed one bit since the last time I saw it." With a pronounced swagger, she approached him. "Still plagued with guilt over Noeh?"

Her words hit him harder than he cared to admit, and a pang squeezed his heart. He was as much a traitor as she. His marking for loyalty burned on his shoulder. He didn't need to look to know that it had faded yet again.

Mauree stepped closer until the tip of her glossy red high-heeled shoe touched the side of his chest. "We want the location of the manual entrance. How difficult an interrogation this becomes is up to you."

The throbbing at his temple flared. There was no way he'd sell his kind for his own hide. He pinched his lips together. "Bite me."

She rammed the tip of her shoe into his ribs. One snapped. He held his breath as the pain washed over him.

"I figured you'd be difficult. That works for me. I do have more than one pointy end on my shoes." Mauree raised her foot. The dark steel rod, a nail showing through the worn-out rubber, glinted in the light.

"Stop!" Kaelyn stepped forward, invading Mauree's personal space. "I said I would interrogate him. After he tricked me into leading him toward the lake house, I deserve my revenge."

Trick her? That was never the plan. Initially, he'd intended to kill her, and that was so much worse, but as he'd led her from the Keep, talked with her, saw her courage and determination, his goal had changed. To what, he wasn't certain, but he never tricked her.

Mauree chuckled. "My, my, if I didn't dislike you so much, I'd find your moxie refreshing. You asked if you could interrogate him, but I never said you'd be *allowed* to. Remember, you work for me, not the other way around."

She waved her hand in a dismissive gesture. "Theron, take her and leave us. My two Gossum friends and I will obtain the information we seek or our prisoner will die in the process."

Saar renewed his struggle against his bindings, drawing on the strength of his beast. He bucked his body against the floor, his muscles straining, yanking the chains again and again.

The bonds held.

Kaelyn lurched toward him, but Theron wrapped his arms around her. She fought as hard as Saar wrestled against his shackles, but like him, she couldn't break free. In the depths of her moist eyes, determination and remorse glittered. His throat constricted.

Theron hauled her from the room, and Saar burned his last image of her into his mind. He'd need it in order to survive.

Theron's fingers dug into Kaelyn's wrist. She struggled against him, but he dragged her from the room and out into the darkening twilight. A blast of spring's cold air hit her on the cheek. Saar's battle to free himself and the look of pure reverence when he'd met her gaze had done her in. She couldn't let them torture him.

"Theron, let me go!"

He crushed her against him, keeping her in place.

She morphed into her bear, the fur growing over her clothing and skin in an instant. Her uncle was unable to contain her, and she broke from his grasp.

"Kaelyn, what are you doing?"

She growled and paced in the grass outside the small cottage. In her bear state, sounds amplified—the whir of a mosquito, the soft flutter of a bat's wings, and through the cracks in the wooden structure, Saar's short, labored breaths and tortured groans.

The muscles in her hind legs tensed. She wanted, no, needed to fight, to burn off some of her frustration, but she wasn't sure who was friend and who was foe, not anymore.

Theron held out his hands and took a tentative step toward her. "Kaelyn, calm yourself. You can't help him this way."

Her long claws dug into the soft soil, and she ripped pieces of grass out by the roots. She'd seen Saar's reaction when she'd said she'd wanted to interrogate him. His brow had furrowed, a flash of surprise crossing his features. His actions were contrary to what Theron claimed—that he'd led her on, toying with her. Perhaps Saar hadn't freed her just to follow her here.

"Come with me." Theron headed along the path that led into the forest.

She followed on padded feet, jogging, and then bursting into a full-on sprint. Energy, quick as liquid, slid through her veins, fueling her muscles. She ran past him, letting her frustration burn itself out before returning. As she morphed into her human state, her pants and T-shirt reformed on her body. Placing her hands on her knees, she leaned over to catch her breath.

"You ready to talk?" Theron reclined against the base of a large oak tree. The gnarled branches reminded her of the Gossum, and she longed to scratch her claws through their dark, emotionless eyes.

Rising from her crouch, she nodded.

He pushed away from the tree and ran his hands down her arms. The comforting gesture was a familiar one. "Good. Now, what exactly is going on here?"

"I...I..." She wasn't sure what to say, what to think. It all sounded so ludicrous.

He placed his finger under her chin and drew her attention to him. "Kaelyn, please. I know something's wrong. Tell me."

He was her uncle, and the one male in this world she trusted without question. "I think...he might be...my mate."

Theron blinked. His eyes flicked back and forth as he studied her then his features hardened. "If you say he's your mate, I believe you."

Her breath hitched in her throat. "I'm going to get him out."

Theron's warm, assuring smile curled his lip. "Somehow, I thought that's where you'd end up. I'll create a diversion. That's the best I can do."

"Thank you." She leaned into him, knowing this might be the last time she ever saw him. Her decision to free Saar put her on a new path. Although she wasn't sure where her choice would lead, this was one gamble she had to take.

Theron gently squeezed her shoulder. "Where will you go? Do you have a plan?"

She smiled. "I have a plan, but it's best I don't share that with you."

A soft chuckle eased from him. "Good. Smart. May the good graces of the gods be with you."

"Thanks, but I'd prefer to take my own chances." Kaelyn had enough of meddling gods to last a lifetime.

$\mathcal{K}$aelyn raised her whistle to her lips and blew. The soft melodic tone eased from the carved wood, informing Theron she was ready. Sensing a better location, she stalked closer to the rear of the cottage and hid behind a large pine. At the edge of the forest, the moon's glow reflected off the bedroom window. Behind the thin curtain, shadows tracked back and forth.

Saar hadn't yelled or screamed, and a measure of respect built in her chest. He was a formidable warrior, one that wouldn't crack under Mauree's torment. A tension headache formed behind her eyes. *Hurry, Theron.*

Insistent footsteps on the cottage's wooden entryway reverberated against the trees. The door banged as it slammed against the frame. Muffled voices from within the cottage grew more agitated. Mauree let out a loud shriek. More shouts followed. Footsteps pounded on the front porch.

Mauree's shrill voice pierced the air. "Farrell, stay here."

"Yes, my lady." A male's low reply.

"Eldon, join me and Theron." Mauree cursed. "Where did you say you saw Zedron?"

"In the kitchen. As soon as I saw the blue mist, I came for you. It's possible..." Theron's voice faded along with the trio's footsteps.

Kaelyn's pulse picked up. Now was her best shot.

She drew her mace from its sleeve, the weight heavy and familiar. With a quick push, she bolted from her hiding spot and ran toward the cottage. Dew coated the short grass, and the damp tips slapped against her ankle.

She crept toward the window and peered between the curtains. The tips of Saar's boots and the manacles that surrounded his ankles came into view. He was motionless, but he still lived. A tendril of hope sprouted in her chest, tiny roots searching for more.

Even with a firm tug, the window remained closed. Locked. *Damn.* "All right, then."

She stepped away and tightened her grip on her mace. Swinging the weapon, she drew it over her head, the force of the heavy ball straining her muscles. The familiar tension bolstered her determination. With a final burst of energy, she smashed the spiked tips against the window.

Glass shattered.

Her pulse quickened as she landed on the windowsill. Careful not to touch any of the sharp glass with her bare hands, she drew herself through and dropped to the wooden floor.

Saar lifted his head. Red welts marred his cheek, his chin, his neck —Gossum stings.

"Kaelyn?" Saar's ragged voice travelled inside, settling into her chest.

She scanned his body for signs of injury. Blood trickled from numerous cuts and scratches over his arms. A large purple bruise bloomed across his chest. Shredded at his calf, his pants clung to his legs.

Blood soaked through the cloth. A red stain marred the wooden floor.

Heat swept up her chest and into her face. She ground her teeth. Using the anger, she swung her mace, around and around, then brought it down on one of the chains at his left ankle. The metal shattered, the small pieces scattering over the smooth floor like marbles.

The door to the bedroom slammed against the wall.

A Gossum stood at the door—Farrell. The hairless skin over his eyes furrowed. "Kaelyn? What are you—"

She didn't wait for him to finish. With a quick flick of her wrist, she yanked a dagger from her belt and launched it at him.

He caught her movement and dodged at the last moment. The blade embedded in his shoulder.

"Watch out!" Saar's voice boomed in the room. The rattling of his chains competed with the Gossum's hiss.

Farrell grabbed the dagger's handle, yanked it from his shoulder then tossed it onto the ground. The tip of his barbed tongue snaked from between his teeth, coming dangerously close to her face.

Kaelyn recoiled and took a step back. Spittle, hot and nasty, landed on her cheek.

She swung her mace at him. The sharp blades left rips in Farrell's shirt but didn't connect with flesh.

Breaking metal pierced the air. She dared not turn her attention away from her opponent.

Farrell's long, pointy claws emerged from his fingertips.

For a brief moment she considered morphing into her bear, but in the confined space, her alter-ego would be more hindrance than help. She doubled down on her determination and held her ground.

A ripping noise, as if something heavy was torn from its foundation, filled the room.

Farrell slashed out with his claws, again and again. She blocked his moves with her mace.

Blood dripped from the wound on Farrell's left shoulder. He favored the limb, protecting it. Using the information to her advantage, Kaelyn struck.

Her ball connected with Farrell's shoulder.

He cried out, but twisted around. His claw grazed down her arm.

Pain raced to her shoulder, fueling her anger.

One last rip, like a boulder crashing against the rocky shore, echoed around the room.

"Get away from her." Saar's voice filled the void.

He stepped forward, dragging his right leg behind him. A shudder wracked his body, and he wavered, but his blue eyes swirled with a beautiful amber, resolve reflecting in their depths.

Her breath bottled up in her throat even as her chest expanded.

They weren't out of trouble yet.

Farrell hissed. "Are you ready to die now?"

"You are mistaken. It is you that shall perish tonight," Saar roared with surprising strength.

Farrell's forearm dangled at an odd angle, motionless against his side, so he raised his good arm, extended his claws, and bolted toward Saar.

Kaelyn swung her mace.

Tongue extended, Farrell launched into the air.

Saar gripped the slippery appendage and yanked the creature toward him.

Kaelyn's mace connected with Farrell's back. The crunch of bone reverberated around the room.

With a quick twist, Saar wrapped the creature's tongue around its own neck and squeezed until the decapitated head slipped from the body. It landed on the floor with a loud thud.

The Gossum's torso disintegrated in Saar's grasp, slipping into a pile of sludge.

"You're alive…" Kaelyn's voice cracked with relief.

Saar wrapped his arms around her. Despite his injuries, he held her with a strength she'd only encountered among her own kind. They didn't have time for this, but she clung to him for a moment, breathing in his scent.

At last, she pulled away. "We should leave, before the others return."

His brow furrowed. "Where is there to go?"

She trailed a finger over the puffy sting mark on his cheek, the one that tracked along his scar.

He flinched at her touch.

With a heavy heart, she drew her hand away, but he stopped her, wrapping his fingers around hers. "I'm sorry. I like the feel of your skin against mine, but no one touches me…there."

His words burrowed deep into her heart, sliding in between the cracks he'd made. This male would be her undoing, of that, she had no doubt.

He's my mate.

The thought struck home. There was no further doubt in her mind. She belonged to him, and he belonged to her.

She swallowed the lump that had formed in her throat. "Trust me. I have the perfect hiding place."

He studied her, his blue eyes searching deep into her soul. "I will follow you wherever you lead."

On a level deep inside, she understood he meant every word. He raised his hand to wipe the sweat from his brow, and a chunk of concrete dangled from the end of the chain. Her gaze tore to his other hand, where another block swung back and forth. At his leg, only a few links of chain remained.

Her stomach twisted. What had they done to him? "Let me remove these. You'll be able to move faster without the added weight."

She picked up her mace.

After kneeling down, he scooted the blocks as far away as he could, stretching the chains taut.

Three dark lines marked the back of his left shoulder blade. *A tattoo?* She didn't have time to dwell on the unusual marks. With one swift move, she launched her mace and crashed the spiked ball onto his bindings.

The links shattered. Shards of broken chain recoiled across the floor as if eager to escape.

A smile tugged at his lip, pulling his scar tight, and a slight dimple formed. She had the urge to kiss the small hollow, but they needed to leave.

She headed for the window, their fastest escape route, but stopped. "Oh, your sword. It's in the other room."

"I'll get it." He disappeared through the doorway, a slight limp to his gait and returned a moment later. With a quick wink, one that made her insides quiver, he sheathed his sword and nodded toward the window. "After you."

She stepped on the sill and hovered on the brink. The drop to the grass was a short distance, but, in so many ways, it was the biggest leap of her life. Without a second thought, she jumped.

Landing on the soft earth, her boots squished into the damp soil. Water pooled along the sole. Saar followed close behind, his movements jilted and slow due to his injuries. Her chest ached for him.

"This way." She gripped his hand and drew him toward the forest. The more distance they put between them and Mauree's minions the better. Funny how she'd come full circle, abandoning her Tribe, her uncle, everything she'd ever known for this male. A twinge tugged at her insides.

"They're gone? Who's responsible for this?" Mauree's shrill voice echoed from the front of the cottage.

A burst of adrenaline urged Kaelyn to run faster over the wet grass. The tree line was only a few feet away. "Hurry, Saar."

"I'm right behind you."

Kaelyn bolted past the trees at the edge of the property, eager for cover.

"Theron! You lied to me. B...betrayed me!" There was no mistaking the anger in Mauree's tone.

From Kaelyn and Saar's vantage point behind the large rhododendrons, the wooden steps leading to the cottage's front porch were bathed in the moon's soft glow.

Shoulders back, head held high, Theron stood in front of Mauree. "...and I'd do so again to help Kaelyn."

Fast as a bullet, Mauree's open palm connected with Theron's face. The skin on skin contact ricocheted through the air. His head whipped to the side. With a quick flick of her wrist, she drew a dagger from a satchel on her thigh. The blade glinted in the moonlight.

Theron gripped his chin, sliding his jaw back and forth. His attention drew to the knife.

Mauree buried the sharp steel in his gut. "No one betrays me and lives. Not even you."

Kaelyn's muscles tensed. *No, no, no.* "Noooo…" The soft wail burst from her lips.

Even as Theron's face reddened, pain etched in the lines around his eyes, he smiled. "Thank you…for freeing me." He slipped to the ground, his body turning to sand.

White spots of rage clouded Kaelyn's vision. She palmed her mace. "I'll kill you. I'll kill you," she whispered roughly.

Saar wrapped his arms around her waist. She strained against him, rage boiling her blood, fueling her need for retribution. Her nails elongated, and she dug them into Saar's arm, leaving a long, bloody scratch. "He's my uncle! Let me go!"

He whipped her around and crushed her against him. With a firm grip, he caught her chin between his fingers. He leaned in and whispered, "Stop, Kaelyn. He gave his life for you. Honor him by living."

She stilled. The glimmer of understanding, acceptance, and love in his beautiful eyes calmed her racing heart. Even though she ached to go after Mauree, he was right. She wouldn't let Theron's sacrifice be in vain.

"Okay, okay," she said, quietly. "But I *will* get my revenge."

Amber flashed through his eyes. "Good. I hope you do. Now, let's go before they see us."

She gripped his hand, and they disappeared into the safety of the forest.

Mauree stared at the pile of sand at her feet. She raised her foot and plowed the pointed end of her high-heeled pump through Theron's remains, scattering the fine grains into the air. A howl of pure rage accompanied her efforts, but neither brought her any satisfaction. Muscles quivering, she lowered her dagger and wiped what remained of his drying blood on the wet grass.

"My lady, how may I assist you?" Eldon stood on the steps to the small cottage. Shoulders tense, he waited for her response.

"Eldon, you've just earned yourself a promotion. Return to the main house and round up a search party. I want Saar and that traitorous bitch found. Now!" Awareness that she was on the edge of madness crept into the back of Mauree's mind, but she didn't care. Not one iota.

"Yes, my lady." Eldon scurried off, his shoes pounding down the path.

Mauree sheathed her dagger and rubbed at her chest, trying to force the building ache to ease. As much as she wanted to love, she was no longer capable, not that she'd ever been, but a sliver of hope had lived in her heart. Not anymore. Theron's betrayal had cut too deep. *I should've known better than to trust him.*

All she'd ever wanted was to be loved by Noeh and to become his queen. Her determination to kill him and win this war for Zedron flared to life like a bonfire, and she used the energy to banish any further thoughts of her traitorous lover from her mind. In its place flowed the bittersweet taste of revenge. "Kaelyn, disloyal little *bitch*, you can't escape me. I'll find you, and when I do, I look forward to hearing you scream."

CHAPTER 23

*K*aelyn came for me and lost her uncle in the process. A mixture of shock, hope, and regret swirled in Saar's gut.

He couldn't process the information, so he concentrated on their trek through the dense foliage. The burn in his shoulder and the ache in his leg pounded along with each beat of his heart, but he refused to let the pain slow him down. His injuries would heal quickly, but not before Mauree and her minions followed them in hot pursuit.

He studied Kaelyn as she traipsed through the dark forest. Stiff back, chin held high, her steps were rushed and forceful.

How she must suffer.

A hole grew in his chest, pain filtering into every nook and cranny. An ache to mirror his own loss. She'd lost her uncle. He'd lost his kind.

Outcasts. Vagrants. Fugitives.

Tracked by both her people and his, they were an island unto themselves with only each other to depend upon.

At least he hadn't disclosed the Keep's entrance during the brutal torture Mauree and her minions had inflicted upon him. He'd bit back a few muffled shouts and a wince or two, but hadn't said a word. Yes, he'd betrayed his kind, but he'd also protected them and that was the best restitution he could give.

Kaelyn's long braid hung down her back. It swayed to and fro with each step, the golden cloth interwoven between the strands. The rhythmic motion captivated him. His hand twitched with his urge to grasp the fine stands between his fingers, pull her to him, kiss her, take away her pain. He reached into his pocket for a toothpick, but came up empty handed.

She stopped next to a pine tree and rested her hand on the bark. Short and rapid, her breaths fogged in the damp air.

He pulled up behind her, listening to the night and the creatures that shared the forest. A cool breeze slid over his skin. The leaves in the trees rustled, as if conversing amongst themselves. He placed his hand next to hers, avoiding skin on skin contact, despite his desire to touch every inch of her body.

With careful attention, he leaned close and whispered in her ear. "Are you okay?"

Her lips parted on a quick intake of breath, and a slow shiver wracked her body.

Empathy for her sorrow constricted his chest. He placed his hands on her shoulders and gave them a gentle squeeze. "Kaelyn—"

She turned toward him. The long length of her braid whipped around, nearly catching him in the face before coming to rest down the front of her shirt. Her gaze scanned the forest around them. "The river isn't far. We'll have to swim downstream, but once we cross, they will lose our scent. Our hiding place is still several miles away. Do you—"

"Stop, Kaelyn. Look at me."

"No, we have to hurry—"

"Shhh..." He placed one finger against her lips.

She tensed.

"Little bear, I'm sorry for your loss. Your uncle must've loved you a great deal."

A stilted hitch burst from her throat. "H...he did, but I can't talk about him, not right now."

"That's understandable. When you're ready, I'll listen." They didn't have time for this conversation, not here, not now, but his burning need to understand overrode common sense. "There's something else I must know."

"What?" Her sweet pea scent worked its way into his lungs, branding her in his mind.

He trailed his fingers over her brow and down her long braid. The soft strands tickled his fingers, endearing her to him. "Why did you return for me?"

The lines around her mouth stiffened, and she raised her chin, putting her lips dangerously close to his. The sexual tension between them sparked, and he half expected the energy to light the sky. "I couldn't let them kill you because..." her throat undulated as she swallowed, "...there's this pull between us. I think you're my mate."

Saar's breath stalled. Adrenaline spiked through his veins, sending a rush of blood south. Before he could process his thoughts, he reacted on impulse, drawing her to him in a bruising kiss. She slid her fingers into his hair and her nails scraped against his scalp with a fevered intensity. The spark between them ignited. He lavished her with kisses, feeding the frenzy between them. When he broke away, her soft panting breaths teased the skin on his chin.

Kaelyn placed her hand on his bicep. "I'd ask if you feel it, too, but I'll take that as a 'yes.' "

He planted a tender kiss on her forehead, giving her his answer. A sudden urgency to flee this place tugged at his insides, his cautious instincts driving him onward. "We should go. You mentioned a hiding place. What do you have in mind?"

"Sometimes it's best to hide in plain sight. We head to the Gossum safe house."

A chill ran over his shoulders. "Tell me you didn't just say that."

Her gaze tracked to the shadows hidden amongst the large trees. "Proves my point. Who would believe we'd go there?"

A part of him wanted to argue with her, but they didn't have time. He exhaled, giving in to her decision. "Little bear, I will follow you wherever you go. Once we get across the river and put some distance between us and your family, we have much to discuss."

She turned her attention to his eyes. The pain and sadness reflected there bore into him.

"Ah, *Craya*, this can't be easy for you." He drew her into his arms, and she leaned into him for a brief moment before pulling away.

"You're right. We need to talk, but..." Kaelyn tensed.

An acrid, astringent scent wafted by on the breeze. *Gossum*.

"Let's go," she whispered.

Before he could respond, she bolted through the trees. As promised, he followed.

CHAPTER 24

$\mathcal{K}$aelyn picked up her pace until she couldn't distinguish between the beat of her boots pounding over the mossy ground and the beat of her heart. Her pants, still wet from the river and their long float downstream, clung to her legs. The shirt was damp, but her hair would take hours to dry in her braid.

At least the water had rinsed off most of the dirt and grime.

She glanced over her shoulder.

Saar still trailed her, his gait stilted from his injury, but he never once complained or asked her to slow. Respect for him swept through her like wildfire, and a lump formed in the back of her throat. She blew out a long exhale and continued toward their unusual haven.

A few minutes later, she crested a hill. A small, rickety cabin loomed in the distance. Moss covered its roof except for a few crumbled shingles near the corner. The front window was broken. A large piece of plywood, boarded from the inside, covered the shattered remains. The desolate place could use some tender loving care.

Saar approached, and the warmth of his presence settled over her.

She wanted to lean into him, soak up his strength, and as if he could read her mind, he wrapped his arm around her waist, encouraging her to rest against him.

"Are we here?" His low voice rumbled in his chest. The vibration travelled deep inside, warming her in places she didn't want to think about.

She smiled. "Yep, this is the Gossum safe house."

"Not much to look at, is it?" He shook his head. "My kind has searched for this place for years. How were you able to find it when we couldn't?"

"Zedron, our illustrious god," she tinged her voice with sarcasm, "has a veil over the cabin. The only reason you can see it now is because you're with me."

He tugged her closer against him. His bicep rubbed across her nipple, teasing her. The bud hardened in response. He leaned down, stubble on his cheek scraping against her neck with delicious friction. "So, you really plan on staying here?"

She squirmed in his embrace. "Why not? It's the ideal hiding spot."

"Ideal? Isn't it overrun with Gossum?" His voice held a hint of apprehension.

"Does it look like Gossum have been here recently?"

He grunted, not convinced.

She turned to face him and peered into his eyes. "Now that they have the lake house, there's no need for them to come here. This is the last place they will look for us."

He searched her features, as if memorizing every detail.

Inside, her wicked traitor of a heart skipped a beat, liking his perusal.

A smile tugged at his lip, stretching the scar tight, but also forming that adorable dimple she was fast coming to love.

"Where you go, I go. Besides," he glanced skyward, "the night will end soon. I must find shelter from the sun."

She wrapped her fingers in his, the rightness of it strengthening the bond growing between them. "Come, then. Let's see what kind of creature comforts they have in there."

He eyed the place again, uncertainty in the creases around his eyes. "I don't relish the idea of staying here, in Gossum territory."

She drew him forward, and they took the overgrown path leading to the place. As they neared, the disrepair became more apparent. The boards near the broken window bulged, warped from countless raindrops. Nestled under the eaves was a bird's nest. Bits of sticks and moss stuck out in all directions, but like the house, no one was home.

With tentative steps, she approached. Even over the musty aroma of mildew and decay, the astringent scent of Gossum permeated the place. The sound of metal scraping against metal rang in the air. She peered over her shoulder.

Saar's mouth was drawn into a thin line. The muscles in his chest flexed as he held his sword. "Let me go first."

"Why? Do you think I can't handle myself with the Gossum? I saved you back there, didn't I? I can do this." She held her breath. This moment, right here, right now, would determine their destiny and dictate how their relationship, if that was what they could call it, would go. Her pulse raced, blood coursing through her veins.

At last, the tautness in his shoulders lessened. A playful smile tugged at his lips. "All right, sassy. After you, then."

She exhaled, the tension easing from her in one long breath. "Thank you."

His brow furrowed. "For what?"

"Trusting me."

Amber flecks swirled in the depths of his blue eyes, and she'd never seen anything more beautiful. Before she got lost in them, she faced the door and nudged it open with her toe. The astringent scent intensified for a moment, then dissipated into the air.

Silence greeted them.

She placed her palm on the handle of her mace for good measure then stepped through the doorway, Saar right on her heels.

Shadows filled the small space, pierced only by the moonlight filtering through the window over the grimy and marred kitchen counter. The only pieces of furniture were an old wooden table and a single kitchen chair. One of the rungs was gone from its back and it reminded her of a mouth with a missing tooth.

Scattered across the warped wooden floor were the remnants of a clock, bits and pieces strewn about in disarray. Stacked in the corner were several opened boxes. Empty Smirnoff bottles stood like miniature soldiers in rows, as if ready for a different kind of battle.

Saar growled, the sound low and predatory. "Disgusting."

"We're not in a position to be choosy." She strode further into the cabin.

Stepping around her, he sheathed his sword. "There's another room."

So caught up in the bottles, she hadn't noticed the open doorway just off the kitchen. She followed him.

A bedroom, except the ragged mattress in the corner looked anything but cozy. She curled her lip, and a growl rumbled in her throat. Who knew what had slept there. There was no other furniture, but a large fireplace graced one wall with a pile of ash in the grate.

Saar's attention drew to her. He held up a finger. "I'll be right back."

With a quick turn, he departed the room. His boots echoed off the old wooden floor and out the door.

She exhaled and laid her mace against the wall. Now that they were done running, she had a moment to think. The silence in the room beat against her psyche. How did she end up here? Two lost souls adrift on a temporary island, alone, together. No place to run, no place to hide.

Bile rose, burning the back of her throat. Where would they go from here? That was a good question, one she couldn't answer.

Her stomach growled, and a wave of nausea accompanied her frustration. *Food.* They needed to eat, especially Saar to help speed his recovery. With a goal in mind and something to focus on other than their situation or her uncle, she returned to the cabin's main room.

The drab kitchen offered a ray of hope. Gossum didn't eat food. Maybe, just maybe, the previous owners had left something behind. She gripped the grime-encrusted handle on the top cupboard and yanked. The door opened with a loud squeak.

Dust sifted to the counter, dislodged after years of collection. Inside, nothing but empty shelves.

A heavy weight settled onto her shoulders. She shrugged it off and continued to the next cabinet. Same result—empty. Faster and faster, she opened the cupboards, searching...hoping...

At last, in the cabinet under the unused and broken sink, she found what she'd longed to find. Two cans sat in the back corner of the bottom shelf. Her chest expanded. She yanked the tins from their hiding spot and placed them on the countertop.

A stifled laugh bubbled from deep inside. Both cans were the same, beef stew. Perfect.

Footsteps echoed on the porch, and she turned in time to catch Saar enter through the doorway. He carried a large bundle of ferns, their green fronds adding a bit of color to the drab surroundings.

"I thought you might like this better than the old mattress." A small smile tugged at his lip, causing the dimple to form.

Her chest constricted. Despite his injuries, he'd picked the plants to make her feel comfortable. The cracks in the walls around her heart widened, crumbling at his unselfish deed. No one had done something so nice for her since Noden.

He hefted the load into the bedroom. When he returned, he headed for the door once again. She placed her hand on his arm, stopping him. Lines formed around his eyes, concern etched in the deep groove between his brows. "What is it?"

His care for her warmed her heart, and she smiled to ease his worry. "Are you hungry? I found some food."

Beautiful gold flecks mixed with the blue in his eyes. "Food? You found food?"

She played on his attempt to lighten the mood and pointed to the counter. "Yes, you have two choices, stew or stew. Which would you prefer?"

A smirk tugged at his lip. "Well, I guess I'll have stew, then."

She picked up one of the cans. "Perfect."

He grabbed the hilt of his sword. "I can open them for you, unless, of course, you found a can opener somewhere."

With a quick flick of her index finger, she extended her claw. "No need. This will do the trick."

His gentle chuckle entwined around her soul.

Happiness at just being with him warmed her on the inside. If only it could last.

CHAPTER 25

*M*auree kept up her pace, the need for vengeance spurning her on. Filtered moonlight fought its way between the forest's thick canopy, and a few hearty rays bathed the ferns and underbrush in its soft radiance. Between the trees, the familiar roar of a river, not too far away, echoed. Somewhere out there was that little bitch, Kaelyn, and the commander turned traitor, Saar.

Mauree stumbled over a rock, the heel of her pump catching on the rough edge as it protruded from the dirt. Hands splayed forward, her palms scraped across the rubble, tearing into her flesh. The scent of blood permeated the air.

"*Craya!*" Her pride injured more than anything else, she rose to her feet. With a quick swipe, she brushed off the bits of moss, dirt, and grime that stuck to her skirt, her blouse, her skin.

A soft chuckle echoed between the trees. Eldon lowered himself from the branches of a nearby pine, squishing some three-leaf clovers along the path's edge.

Mauree raised her chin. "What are you laughing at?"

A slow smile curled his lip. "Not a thing, my lady, not a thing."

Another Gossum slipped from the tree to join Eldon. A few more scurried up the path behind her, along with a handful of Ursus warriors.

Mauree wiped her bloody palm down the side of her skirt. "Are we close to finding them yet?"

Eldon bowed low, but his dark eyes never left hers. "No, but we haven't lost the trail—"

"Then let's continue." Mauree strode forward, invading Eldon's personal space. His astringent smell burned the hairs in her nose, but the acrid scent was as bitter as her heart, reinforcing her desire to bring Kaelyn down. The bitch had convinced Theron to help her escape, and in the process Mauree had lost her favorite play thing.

Payback was in order, big time.

Eldon stepped back. "As you wish, my lady."

Mauree's jaw stiffened. "Good. Lead on."

Eldon disappeared down the trail, his companions close behind. Mauree glanced at her palm. Blood dribbled from the small gash. She clenched her fingers into a fist. *Damn you, Theron.*

Once Mauree found Kaelyn, death would be fast and efficient.

A rush of energy, fueled by anger, shot her muscles into gear, and she followed the Gossum deeper into the forest.

The rushing of water over boulders grew louder with each step. Mauree burst past a large rhododendron bush to stand at the river's edge.

Muscles tense with strain, Eldon hunched near the water's edge, his nose quivering as he scented the air. He pointed at one of his brood. "You, search upstream."

The male nodded, then scampered along the bank, sniffing the air as he ran.

Eldon eyed the remaining soldiers. "The rest of you, search downstream."

In a matter of moments, Mauree and her new first lieutenant were alone.

Mauree placed her hands on her hips. "Don't tell me you lost them."

Eldon stared at her, his dark orbs reflecting the moonlight like glass. "Then I won't, but I suspect they went for a swim."

"To lose us, no doubt." Mauree huffed. "Lovely."

Eldon's gaze tracked over Mauree's blouse and skirt. "Looks to me like you could use a swim, wash off some of that dirt you accumulated from your little, uh...spill."

Mauree growled. "Are you trying to annoy me?"

The skin on his forehead crinkled. "Of course not, my lady, just stating—"

"Your task is to find Kaelyn and Saar. Nothing else. Got it?"

His features hardened. "My point, if you'd allow me make it, is that we'll have to cross the river to continue our search. That is, unless you'd rather return to the lake house."

She glowered at him. "I'm well aware they most likely crossed the river. A swim is a small price to pay to find them."

The Gossum who'd ventured upstream returned. He skidded to a stop, his tongue whipping back and forth with his excitement. In his hands, he held a broken manacle. "I found this buried in a crevasse between a couple of boulders along the river's edge. Saar must've busted this off before entering the river."

Eldon clapped the male on the shoulder. "Well done. You've confirmed our suspicions. Now, gather the others. We cross here."

"As you command." The male smiled, revealing his serrated teeth. A thin line of spittle dripped from his lip before he loped downstream.

Bile filled Mauree's mouth, and she peered at Eldon. "Your kind is so...disgusting."

Eldon raised an eyebrow. "Each to their own, my lady." He turned his attention to the trees on the other side of the river. "We'll have to scout the bank for quite a ways before we pick up their trail again."

"I have faith in your abilities. We will find them. No other outcome is acceptable." Blood from Mauree's clenched fist dripped onto a rock at her feet, staining the surface crimson.

CHAPTER 26

$\mathcal{K}$aelyn tapped her finger against the kitchen sink and stared out the grime-encrusted window. Deep purple colored the sky, the first indication daybreak would soon chase away the night. She gripped her whistle. The comforting weight helped calm her nerves, but only a little. *Where are you, Saar?*

As if he'd heard her thoughts, his footsteps echoed off the cabin's small entryway. The door opened with a slight squeak.

Kaelyn sighed, tension draining from her shoulders. He'd returned, safe and sound.

With a Smirnoff's bottle in each hand, he strode into the room. His eyes gleamed with triumph.

She laughed, unable to resist his charm. "I see you found the stream."

He raised an eyebrow, mirth toying at the corner of his mouth. "Have faith, little bear, I can slay water better than any warrior you know."

She had no doubt of his ability, having seen him battle first hand. He'd defeated four Gossum before Theron, Jacinth, and she had finally brought him down. He was a warrior among warriors. A flutter of pride beat against her chest.

As he crossed the room, she took the opportunity to assess his wounds. The limp in his stride was less pronounced, the bruise on his side fading to a light yellow, the gash on his forehead a thin scab. Satisfied with his improvement, her attention turned to his broad, muscular chest. She wanted to run her fingers over his soft flesh, feel the taut, corded muscles beneath her palms. A growl of pure admiration scraped the back of her throat.

He sidled up next to her and placed the bottles on the counter. The tattoo on his shoulder blade caught her attention—three jagged black lines, like claw marks. One was dark, the other two seemed faded. She opened her mouth to ask him about them, but he spoke first.

"Ah, stew," he inhaled with a long, slow breath, "what a treat."

She smiled. "Indeed, a meal fit for a pair of vagabonds like us."

His features softened, the mirth in his eyes dimming. He studied her for a moment then twirled his finger around a loose curl that had escaped her braid.

A needful tremor ran along her arms.

"You're cold." His attention drew down her body before returning to her face. Desire and concern mixed with the amber in his blue eyes. "Your pants are still wet from the river."

So focused on settling into this place, she hadn't noticed, but now that he mentioned it, the damp clothes clung to her legs. An unbidden shiver travelled up her back and over her shoulders, leaving goosebumps in its wake.

He trailed his finger down her arm, adding a tingle to the sensitive skin. "You need warmth. I'll be right back."

With a quick turn, he headed for the door.

"Where are you going?"

Stopping, he peered at her over his shoulder. "There's a woodpile on the side of the cabin. Most of the logs are rotten, but I'll bet I can find enough salvageable pieces to make a decent fire."

Before she could protest she didn't need him to care for her, he was gone. *Damn it.* She clenched her jaw. All her adult life she'd done things for herself, but this male had weaseled his way under her skin from the moment they'd met.

She exhaled, grabbed the two bottles of water, the two cans of now-opened stew, and a couple of spoons she'd found in a drawer. Cradled in her arm, one of the bottles almost slipped, but she made it into the room without mishap and placed her loot on the fireplace mantel.

In the grate, a few small pieces of charred wood poked through the ashes, remnants of a fire long ago. Ferns, one on top of another, graced the edge of the stone hearth, laid out with a meticulousness that spoke of tenderness and caring.

Her throat constricted. Saar had done that for her.

She bent down and touched the cool fronds.

Their fresh scent wafted into her lungs, resurfacing memories of her youth. Many a time she'd frolicked in the ferns with Noden, his teasing play full of love and affection. Warmth from his memory filled her chest.

How she missed her brother, and now her uncle, too, was gone.

The front door squeaked, drawing her from her reverie. Saar's footsteps echoed in the empty room. He appeared in the bedroom doorway, arms full of wood, small twigs, and moss.

Eager to assist him, she wrapped her fingers around two of the logs and tossed them next to the fireplace.

He knelt on one knee and placed the remaining pieces onto the pile. As his shoulders flexed, the mark on his back rippled.

Her breath hitched. "Why do you have that tattoo?"

Tension tightened his shoulders for a moment then he turned to look at her. His mouth thinned, and a pained expression crossed his features. "It's a long story."

Between the drab curtains, the first rays of the morning sun lit a small line along the floor. "The sun is up. Seems like we're here for the day. I have lots of time."

He raised his arm and ran his fingers along the edge of the mantle. With a quick wink, he held up his hand, a match pinched between his thumb and forefinger. "Looks like this is our lucky day."

He placed moss and small twigs into the fireplace, and before long, a fire crackled in the hearth.

A stiff breeze rattled the windows. The wind would carry the smoke through the dense forest, keeping them hidden.

Still crouched, Saar turned toward her and patted the ferns in invitation. "Come, sit with me. Warm yourself."

The low rumble of his voice called to her on a level so deep, she couldn't stop herself. She handed him the two bottles of water from the mantle then grasped the stew and sat next to him. At some point, they needed to talk about their future, or lack thereof, but she wasn't ready. All she wanted was to enjoy his company, at least for a little while.

They ate in silence for a moment, only the sound of the spoons clinking against the metal cans and the crackling of the fire filling the air. She peered at him, but he seemed distant, focused on the flames.

He took a long drink from the bottle then cleared his throat.

"The lines over my shoulder blade are not a tattoo. When born, every Stiyaha male receives a mark on his skin representing the values most important to that male. Often, one or more are tested during his lifetime." A slow, stilted laugh emerged from his throat. "I thought mine had already been tested when I received my scar. I was wrong."

She placed her empty can and spoon on the floor then ran her fingers down his forearm until her hand rested in his. She gave him a gentle squeeze. "One of your marks represents courage, doesn't it?"

His eyelid twitched, and he clasped her hand in confirmation.

"That doesn't surprise me. What about the other two? What values do they symbolize?"

He pulled his gaze to hers. The light from the fire reflected in the depths of his eyes, along with his pain and regret. A lump formed in her throat, and she swallowed, forcing it down. How bad could it be?

A twinge crossed his features. "Honor and loyalty. Both of which I've failed."

She flinched at the harshness in his tone. "I don't believe it."

"My loyalty has always been to my king and my kind. The faded marks reveal the truth. I am no longer a loyal and honorable male."

She furrowed her brow. "From what I've seen, you've been nothing but honorable and loyal, helping me—"

"That's what you think, but you're wrong."

She jerked her hand from his grasp. "What do you mean?"

"When I pulled you from your cell," he ran his hand through his hair, "it wasn't to release you."

Her heart fluttered, picking up speed. "You did it on purpose...to follow me, find Mauree's hideout. Didn't you?" Theron was right. Saar had played her for a fool.

A low, deprecating chuckle eased from him. "No, it was much worse than that."

Her pulse pounded in her ears. "Tell me."

"My task was to kill you."

He reached for her, but she scrambled off the ferns and over the dirt-encrusted floorboards, putting some distance between them.

A rush of adrenaline spiked through her veins. White spots formed in her vision. "No. No. No."

Pain etched itself into the lines on his face. "I couldn't complete my task in front of Ginnia, so I took you outside, but when the time came, I couldn't follow through. I betrayed my king and everyone in the Keep for you...and, *craya*, despite it all, I wouldn't change a thing."

The words penetrated through the fog in her mind. He'd sacrificed everything for her. An ache built in her chest, the pain filtering into the deepest recesses of her soul. "Why did you follow me?"

"Because I couldn't let you go. I knew in here," he pounded his chest, "that you were my mate."

Her throat constricted, pain radiating from the tightness. After rolling from her sitting position to her hands and knees, she crawled toward him.

Rigid and still, he tracked her movements, as if afraid of her reaction.

Mere inches from him, she stopped, their gazes meeting, each assessing the other. Saar loved her, cared for her. She knew that deep inside. This strong, proud male was as honorable as they came, and she loved him more than she could say. "I'm glad you followed me."

With a possessiveness that took her breath away, he hauled her onto his lap.

At his sudden move, she inhaled. He took advantage of her surprise and kissed her, claiming her with an intensity that sparked her own. She growled and dug her claws into his back, leaving a jagged scratch on his right shoulder to match the one on his left, marking him in her own way.

CHAPTER 27

Saar's inner beast roared, and he couldn't stop the growl that rumbled in his chest. Seated across his lap, Kaelyn's soft bottom pressed against his thighs. This tough, feisty female who hid her insecurities beneath her rough exterior had wormed her way into his heart, and underneath the shell she wore like a badge of honor, she was tender, loving.

He vowed to bring that side out, no matter the consequences. More likely than not, today would be their only time together, and he didn't want to waste a moment with her.

His erection strained against his pants, the material cutting into his balls, squeezing them to the point of pain. He groaned and rasped, "Kaelyn, I can't get enough of you."

She placed her forehead against his, her soft breaths caressing the skin on his cheek. A soft sigh eased from her lips. "That's a good thing."

A rush of blood headed south, straining his already engorged shaft. "Ah, little bear…"

Kaelyn leaned back, her eyes flitting back and forth as she studied him. Her attention flicked to his scar then returned to his eyes. "May I…touch it?"

He knew what she meant, and his breath bottled in his throat. No female had ever wanted to touch him, not there, and that she did spoke volumes about her character. Surprisingly, his usual urge to shove a toothpick in his mouth was gone. Swallowing the centuries' long impulse to deny her request, he gave her a quick nod.

She focused on his scar and her finger, soft and tender trailed over the taut skin.

Damn if he didn't like her touch, his arousal jumping as if she'd caressed his erection instead of his face.

With tender care, she followed the thick trail from his cheek, over his upper lip, and around his chin. "It's softer than I imagined." Her gentle words bore into him, burying into his soul.

"Is this what you meant when you said you thought you'd already been tested?"

His throat was so tight he couldn't respond, so he gave her another nod.

Something that looked eerily similar to respect flashed in her eyes. "How did it happen?"

His already rapid pulse notched up a level. "Noeh and I stayed behind our outdoor class to watch a couple of bucks fight. That was my fault, I encouraged him to remain with me." He licked his lips, and her eyes riveted on them, her pupils dilating.

The sudden urge to kiss her again raced through him. He tugged her close. She didn't resist, and he kissed her with a bruising intensity, one born of all the passion he'd bottled up inside. After a long moment, she pushed against his shoulders, breaking the kiss.

"I want to hear the rest, please, before I can't think straight."

The muscle in his arm trembled, his need to make love to her competing with his desire to honor her request. He exhaled. "Gossum arrived. We fought. One raced toward Noeh. He didn't see it coming. I jumped in the way. The creature sliced its claw across my face before I killed it, but not before Noeh was injured."

She inhaled. "But, he lived. You saved him."

Frustration rippled along his nerves. "He was in a coma for a week.

It was my fault the Gossum found us in the first place. I dishonored him and myself."

"He chose to go with you, didn't he?" Her lips pursed as she studied him. "You aren't responsible for his choice."

Noeh almost died because of you.

His father's words echoed in his mind, reinforcing the guilt that plagued him. A hard ball formed in his gut. Suddenly, he wanted to stand, escape her interrogation, and he gripped his fingers around her waist to move her.

Kaelyn placed her hands over his. "Please, don't. I want to stay right here, with you."

The muscles in his arms tensed.

She didn't reject him.

In that moment, the connection between them solidified into an unbreakable bond.

Saar couldn't breathe. White spots threatened behind his eyes.

"Saar, look at me." Her tender words were like an anchor, and he followed them from the depths as if they were his lifeline.

A ragged, rough breath burst from him.

She smiled and placed her lips on his cheek, near the edge of his scar. Her gaze flicked to his, and she held it as she trailed soft, gentle kisses along the marred tissue. When her mouth reached his, she closed her eyes, the elegant lashes gracing her creamy features, so clean, so unblemished, so unlike his own.

A shameless groan slipped from him as her light, feathery lips skimmed over his, teasing him. After a long moment, she continued along her chosen path, leaving soft kisses in her wake. At the base of the scar, she lingered a tad longer, pressing her lips firmly against his chin before peering into his eyes once again.

Her eyes glimmered with a caring appreciation he'd never seen before. His chest tightened around his heart, but there was no protection left. She'd broken through his barriers, owning him, claiming him completely. Where once stood a gaping hole now resided an undeniable love for a female that had stolen his heart.

"I think we shall have to agree to disagree on that topic." Her voice brought him out of his trance.

His brain fogged. "What topic?"

A delightful giggle eased from her lips.

The sound was like a boon to his battered soul.

From outside, a loud crash echoed through the trees.

Kaelyn jumped, pulling away from him to a standing position in one quick move. She bolted to the window. He followed right behind, but before he could stop her, she peeked through the edge of the curtain. A beam of sunlight glowed against her skin.

He tensed. Visions of her flesh burning raced through his mind, but nothing happened. Then, he remembered…she's on Zedron's team. A crushing pain hit him in the chest.

No, she wasn't the enemy, not anymore.

She was his.

CHAPTER 28

Kaelyn's pulse pounded in her ears, her senses on high alert. She tugged the edge of the curtain just enough to peer outside. The trees, lit by the morning sun, stood like sentries. How she wished that were true. The forest was still. There wasn't even a slight breeze to rustle the leaves. A knot formed in her gut. Had they been discovered?

She turned to face Saar.

He clenched his fist around the hilt of his sword. Even in the dull light filtering through the curtain's material, the blade glinted. The muscles in his well-defined chest were tight, and the tic in his jaw pulsed in a steady rhythm. "What do you see?"

"Nothing. But that doesn't mean anything." She stepped away from the curtain, grabbed her mace from its resting spot against the wall, and headed into the other room.

As she passed Saar, he gripped her arm. "Where are you going?"

She bristled under his tone and tore her arm from his grasp. "To have a look."

"No."

She clamped her jaw so tightly, pain reverberated up the side of her face. "One of us needs to. I can go in the sun. You can't. Easy decision."

A slow growl eased from between his lips, and she could've sworn the hair on his arm lengthened for a moment. "I don't like the idea of you going out there, alone."

Deep inside, she understood he wanted to protect her. She'd had enough of males trying to do that and dying in the process, first her brother then her uncle. "Neither do I, but there's no other choice and no time to debate this."

She turned to go, but he stopped her once again. He wrapped his arm around her waist, and he brought her to him. Her hands landed on his bare chest, her fingers tingling from the contact.

The warm scent of pepper and lime wrapped around her, cocooning her in his heady scent.

"Come back to me." His voice was deep and gravelly with a promise of something more.

"The sooner you let me go, the faster I'll return." She glared at him, but her gaze slid to his mouth. The sudden urge to kiss him, to feel the passion burn inside her once again, tingled her lips.

He released her, and her heart skipped a beat. By letting her go, he'd given her his trust, treated her like an equal. Respect for him bloomed in her chest.

With a slow twist, she opened the door a crack then scooted onto the small porch.

A search of the area revealed a wolf who had taken down a deer. The poor creature had almost run when he'd spotted her, recognizing her as the alpha predator.

She'd backed away, letting him know she wasn't interested in his kill. Then, quickly, she'd returned to the cabin as promised.

She slid inside and found Saar positioned near the door, sword raised ready for battle. He lowered his weapon, sheathing it with one swift motion.

"It was a wolf. We're alone. There's no one out—"

He drew her into his embrace. "Thank the gods you're all right." The muscles in his arms shook.

She placed her head on his chest, basking in his warmth.

He brushed his fingers down her long braid, the sensation prickling her scalp, relaxing her. His heart beat a steady rhythm beneath her ear.

She wanted to stay here in his arms, in this small sanctuary, forever, but that was impossible. They only had today. She'd make the most of every minute.

With a new sense of urgency, she stepped back, gripped his hand and tugged him toward their makeshift bedroom. "Let's go back to the fire."

A sexy smile formed on his lips, and warmth pooled at the juncture between her legs. She urged him forward, her steps rushed.

Alone at the fire once again, she threw a log onto the dying flames, a sudden shyness overcoming her. It had been several years since she'd last been with a male.

As if sensing her discomfort, he slid his arm around her waist, but didn't pressure her.

"Tell me about this." He brushed his fingers over the bear's head whistle nestled in the slight "V" at her chest.

Her fingers rose to her favorite piece, the memories flooding her mind. "Noden...my brother. We each carved one, a matching set to honor the bears, our sacred symbol here on Earth. He taught me how to blow through the holes, use the different sounds as a code."

"Will you show me?" His voice was low, reverent.

She glanced into his eyes. Soft pools of blue, they swam with compassion and encouragement. A lump formed in her gut, fastening into a knot.

She brought the whistle to her lips, placing her fingers over the holes in the bear's ears and nose, and with experience honed through time, she blew lightly through the opening. A soft melody emitted from the bear's mouth, and as she uncovered the hole over one of the ears, the tone softened. "That is the sound for 'come to me.'"

"Very beautiful. Is there more?" His interest in her small instrument took her breath away.

No one had paid this much attention to the small bauble since...

not since Noden. A painful, familiar ache burned in her chest. She brought the carved symbol of their kind to her lips and blew three times. The short staccato notes, equal in rhythm and pitch, reverberated off the walls.

As he smiled, the scar pulled tight across his face. She'd never seen anything so beautiful as the pure joy reflected there.

When he spoke, his words were low, reverent. "What does that signify?"

"That is the sign for 'danger.'" Sharing the sacred calls seemed like the most natural thing in the world, as if he were part of them, as if he belonged.

"You mentioned your brother gave you this." He brushed his fingers over the yellow scarf in her braid. "Tell me more about him."

She exhaled, unsure about how much she wanted to say. "He's dead."

"I'm sure you miss him, very much." His words stroked the sore spot in her soul and tears formed in her eyes.

"I do. Every day. He taught me everything, looked out for me, cared for me." Her voice choked, and she couldn't continue. A tear slipped onto her cheek, then another.

"You were lucky to have him. I'm sorry for your loss." He cupped her chin in his palm and wiped away the moisture with his calloused thumb. The roughness of his skin teased her cheek, and she leaned into him, seeking his comfort.

He pressed his lips against her forehead, the kiss tender and loving. With deliberate slowness, he brushed his lips over each eyelid, then down the bridge of her nose. At last, his lips met hers. His kisses were gentle at first, but soon became more intense, and she gripped his shoulders, pulling him close.

When he released her, he ran his fingers down her braid until he came to the knot at the end. "May I undo this?"

The memory of him asking her to unbraid her hair in the Keep's cell resurfaced full force. The reason then...to release her from her physical cell. The reason now...to release her from her mental one.

They'd come a long way since then, and without a doubt, she'd fallen for him. "Yes. I'd like that, very much."

With a reverence and tenderness she'd fast grown to love, he untied the knot and slipped his fingers through her braid, unraveling each twist with slow, deliberate strokes, as if prolonging the task as long as possible, relishing in it. Tears threatened to fall again. She blinked them away, not wanting to blur her vision and miss this special moment.

He toyed with the hair at her nape, and her long strands hung down to her waist.

She'd always had thick, full hair, and the braid was the only way to contain the unruly tresses. Even now, several hours after their arrival, her hair was still damp from their swim in the river.

He trailed his fingers through her locks once more, then placed her scarf in her palm, closing her hand around the material.

His tender gesture broke through her walls. She couldn't contain the tears any longer. They spilled from her eyes, and she wiped them away with the cloth.

He stroked her arms, his warm, strong hands, giving her the comfort and support she'd so desperately wanted all her life.

She inhaled, forcing herself to calm, her grip tightening around her treasured braiding cloth. She placed her hand on the back of Saar's, encouraging him to turn it over. When he did, she tugged at his fingers, opening them for her, and she placed her scarf in his palm.

His eyes widened. "What are you doing?"

"I want you to have this." Her words came out rough, breathy, but she couldn't help it.

He shook his head and pushed the cloth toward her. "I can't take your scarf from you. This—"

"—is my gift to you. Would you refuse me?"

He swallowed, the knot at his throat rising and falling. "I...I...don't know what to say."

She wrapped the long strand around his wrist and created a short knot on the end. " 'Thank you' seems appropriate."

A soft, chuckle, deep and masculine, rose from him. "Thank you, little bear, but I have another, more personal, way I'd like to express my gratitude."

She closed the gap between them and ran her fingers over his shoulder. "Well then, by all means, thank me."

CHAPTER 29

Saar gripped Kaelyn around the waist, tugging her close to his chest. Warmth from the fire chased away the chill in the air and cast a warm glow over Kaelyn's features. He wrapped his hand around the base of her neck. The yellow scarf around his wrist reflected against the velvety skin at her throat, revealing just how vulnerable she was to him and how much she'd given him with her gift—trust, acceptance, love.

His chest constricted, squeezing the breath from him, but he couldn't hold back, and he gave her a bruising kiss. Her hair grazed the back of his hand, his bicep, his chest. The long strands seemed to be everywhere, surrounding him in all that was Kaelyn.

She let out a possessive, demanding moan.

His little bear was everything he needed.

Her admiring gaze tracked over his chest and down to his waist. A soft growl emerged from her lips along with a flash of fang. "Seems you have a head start on me. Why am I still dressed?"

He chuckled, his chest warming from her words. "I can take care of that for you, if you'd like."

She nodded. "I'd like that very much."

With a swift move, he gripped the bottom of her shirt. She raised her hands, and he drew the thin material over her head. It landed on the wooden floor with a soft whoosh. Her bra, dark as night, accentuated the creaminess of her skin. He trailed a solitary finger along the strap and over the lip of the cup. With deliberate slowness, he rubbed his finger down the soft cleavage between her full and heavy breasts.

She gripped his forearms, a shiver wracking her body. "That feels good."

"There's more to come, little bear, I promise." He brushed his finger up the other side, following the cup's contour and over the strap. As he leaned forward, he slid his fingertips down her back and unhooked the clasp. Drawing the material forward, he exposed her luscious breasts to him for the first time. The bra slipped from his fingers, landing at their feet.

He held his breath, admiring her beauty. With tender care, he stroked his finger down her soft skin and cupped one breast in his palm. The heavy weight sent a surge of blood to his groin, straining his already hard shaft. A groan ripped from his throat.

Kaelyn tugged at his pants, pressing the material tighter against his erection.

He gripped her wrist in her palm. "Not yet."

Saar's inner beast growled, eager to take her right here, right now, but he wouldn't, not that way. He wanted to take his time, enjoy her, savor her for as long as they had together.

She pouted, her pretty lips pursing for him.

He drew her to him, kissing her, possessing her, owning her. The sac under his tongue hardened, filling with his bonding ink. The urge to release the fluid pounded along with his heartbeat, but he resisted. Now was not the time, not yet. Breaking their kiss, he worked on her pants. The zipper released with a loud rip.

Helping him, she wiggled her way out of her trousers, kicking off her boots, underwear, and socks in the process. The entire heap ended up with the shirt. She grabbed the bra nestled between her toes, twirled it above her head, and tossed it onto the pile.

Naked before him, she was absolutely beautiful. She leaned forward, and he raised his hand. "Wait. Let me admire you first."

A blush crept up her chest and into her cheeks, coloring her skin a lovely pink shade.

He chuckled. "I had no idea you had a shy streak. My, my."

She crossed her arms over her chest, blocking his view of her beautiful breasts. When he gave her a chagrinned smile, her eyes sparked, and she trailed her hand down his arm. With a determination he knew better than to get in the way of, she laced her finger in the loop of his belt and tugged on the buckle.

Adept and quick, she had him undone in a matter of moments.

His member jutted over the opening, relief flooding him at the release from his confinement. He heeled off his boots and removed his pants, tossing them aside. As he stood, a low, feminine gasp rose into the air.

Saar glanced at her.

Kaelyn drew her attention from his crotch to his eyes. "Um, wow, just, wow."

His chest filled with pride. "You like what you see?"

Kaelyn nodded and wrapped her fingers around his hard member.

An involuntary shiver of delight wracked his body, and a slow moan escaped his lips. "You're killing me."

For a moment darkness crossed her features, but then it faded, her smile returning. Releasing him, she placed her hands around his neck. As if she wanted to erase his words from his mouth, her demanding, fevered kiss bore into him.

She guided him toward the ferns he'd laid out for her to sleep on. Initially, he hadn't planned on joining her, intent only on watching over her, and protecting her instead, but he was lost to her now. He helped her down to her knees, never letting her slip from his embrace. The fronds were soft, fresh, a carpet of greenery to cushion them from the hard floor.

Once on the supple leaves, both kneeling, he stopped their descent and cupped her chin in his palm. Kaelyn's eyes glimmered in the fire's soft glow, the golden flames dancing in the hazel-green. She smiled, and his heart softened, burning the vision of her lovely face into his mind. Her breasts pressed into his chest, her round, hard nipples lighting up his skin. Strands of her hair tickled his bicep, his hip, his thigh, driving his need for her.

Mine. The single word reverberated in his head with a growl. The beast knew what he wanted...Kaelyn. Saar couldn't hold back any longer. He gripped her bottom, compressing her against him. His hot and hard erection pulsed along the smooth contours of her stomach.

She inhaled, then sighed on a long exhale.

Saar placed his hand at the base of her neck and claimed her mouth, licking the seam between her lips. As she opened to him, he deepened the kiss, his tongue sliding along hers with delicious friction. The scent of sweet peas permeated the air, mixing with the aroma of burning cedar.

His shaft twitched with need, desire, and want for her. A growl eased from him, part frustration, part demand.

"Is something wrong?" Her breath came out in short, quick pants.

"I smell your arousal, little bear." He pulled her closer, bringing her cheek to rest against his chest. With deliberate slowness, he trailed his hand down her back, over her long, soft tresses, until he came to rest at the juncture between her southern cheeks. "Spread your legs for me."

She inhaled, tensing in his arms for a moment before relaxing once again. The scent of her need thickened. A soft sigh escaped her lips, and she complied with his demand, spreading her legs.

He slid his finger down her crease and between her slick passage. Her slippery wetness coated his skin. A moan escaped her lips, the vibration traveling from her chest to his, lighting up his senses.

He swirled his fingers along her delicate folds, wet and glossy with her arousal. Every third circle, he graced her clit, the little bud hardening under his ministrations. He tortured her for several long moments before dipping his finger into her cleft. Her sheath tightened around him.

His bonding sac hardened to the point of pain, and a groan of pure frustration eased from his throat. "Kaelyn, will you bond with me?"

"What?" she croaked.

"Little bear, will you be my mate?"

She moaned, writhing against his finger, matching the rhythm of his strokes. "I thought I already was."

Pride expanded in his chest, filling him with love for his precious Kaelyn. He couldn't speak, the words bottled up in his throat. Placing a finger under her chin, he drew her gaze to meet his.

Glossy and dark, her eyes spoke of her passion, her desire, her love for him.

Saar brought his lips to hers, and as he stroked her with his finger, he slid his tongue between her lips. She groaned under his onslaught, and before he could change his mind, question the rationality of his decision, he bit down on his bonding sac.

Ink filled his mouth, and as he kissed her, he gave her his heart along with his silky fluid. He crossed a line he could never come back from. She owned him, now and forever. When he broke the kiss, his shaft pulsed sensitive and hard against her abdomen.

Kaelyn's rough panting grew to a fevered pitch while he continued to pleasure her. At last, she stiffened in his embrace, a shudder of pure feminine bliss pulsing through her, tying him to her as only she could.

∾

White spots flitted across Kaelyn's vision. Her legs trembled, quivering as the last pulse of her orgasm ran its course. Still on her knees with her head resting on his chest, she melted into Saar, enjoying his masculine scent and the fragrance of her arousal.

Saar withdrew his finger and gripped her thigh, her skin slick with her arousal. The erotic nature of it sent a fresh round of wetness to her core.

Long and hard, his erection pressed against her stomach. She choked out her words. "Saar, I want you, inside me."

With a quick roll, he lay on the ferns, hauling her on top of him.

Her hands landed on his firm pecs, and she enjoyed how his taut muscles flexed beneath her fingers. Straddling his hips, the inside of her thighs compressed against his waist.

The hot length of his member pulsed against her buttocks and lower back. His hips undulated, moving with his hunger.

Need reflected in the depths of his eyes. Hooded and dark, they bore into her, reaching into the deepest recesses of her heart. Walls that once protected the precious organ, shattered.

I love him... Admitting this was easier than she'd expected, the truth of it soothing her battered heart. *...and now I'm his mate.*

Letting the tenderness he elicited in her soul flow through her hands, she ran her fingers over his strong pecs and biceps, enjoying his inner strength beneath the softness of his skin. That he hid the compassion in his heart around his rough exterior wasn't lost on her.

She leaned forward and planted a kiss on his lips, pouring all her love for him into their embrace.

He responded to her, the passion between them sparking to a new level she didn't know was possible. When he released her, she raised her hips and centered herself over him.

With deliberate slowness, she lowered herself onto his length, her body stretching to accommodate his size, which filled her with a delicious fullness.

"Are you all right?" The concern in his voice just about broke her.

A tightness formed in her throat. He was so caring, so loving, she didn't deserve him. "I'm fine. Just need a moment."

Although he nodded, apprehension remained etched in the lines around his eyes.

She tickled the fine hairs on his lower abdomen. "Don't worry. You're not hurting me."

Saar held her gaze for a moment before his features relaxed, but there was something in his eyes she couldn't quite put her finger on.

She lowered herself further and started moving, slow and steady at first then building in tempo. He gripped her hips, taking control, slowing her for a moment then increasing his speed. His jaw pulsed, pulling the scar taut across his lip, reminding her of his tale. He was an honorable male even if he didn't believe it himself.

Her excitement built along with his until her orgasm broke free. She floated on a wave of ecstasy, carried along by his love for her and hers for him. He followed close behind, holding her still as he climaxed. After a long moment, he held out his arms and she lay on his chest. In his embrace, she discovered warm comfort. She knew deep in her soul that this was where she belonged. As she relaxed against him, exhaustion threatened to send her into a peaceful sleep.

Sooner or later, reality would crash down on them, but not today...not today.

CHAPTER 30

The stars over Lemuria twinkled as if taunting Alora, teasing her, telling her they were her only companions in the sky until the war over Earth was won. She pushed away from the window and let out a huff. She'd stewed all day in her dark place, nothing to do but think about the war, her choices, and her latest discovery, thanks to Carine.

She curled her fingers around Zedron's recording device and tapped her closed fist against the edge of her visus bacin. The impact sent a ripple across the water's surface, lapping at the edge of the bowl like tiny waves.

"What do I do?" Her words filled the empty room, absorbing into the Rolmdew tree's inner bark.

Don't take matters into your own hands. Veromé's voice echoed in her mind.

A frustrated scream threatened to escape, and she pounded her fist against the bowl's hard surface, again and again. Pain radiated through her hand, but she didn't care. She wanted to lash out at Zedron, make him pay for all the hurt and pain he'd brought into her life.

The war on Earth wasn't about the water, not really, not for him.

Petty and vindictive, he'd do just about anything to get back at her for not choosing him as her mate.

A shiver ran over her shoulders. At least she'd made the right choice. Veromé loved her without question.

The ripples in the water slowed. Time to check on the war, see how the game fared.

She tucked the small disc into the lining along her waistband. Closing her eyes, she glided her palms over her visus bacin, slowly at first, then faster and faster. The water bubbled, gaining momentum, until the roar echoed around the room like drums.

She stilled and opened her eyes.

The water calmed, unlocking a window upon Earth. A picture emerged. Evergreen trees lit by the soft glow of the setting sun. The cool scent of cedar wafted into her senses. She inhaled, enjoying the sweet fragrance. Not far away stood a ramshackle old cabin. A wood-pile, most of the pieces falling apart and rotten, graced one side of the wooden structure. Smoke curled from the chimney, adding to the scents in the air.

The image zoomed in, taking her through the bedroom window. Inside, two figures lay on a mat of ferns near the fire, a male and a female. They seemed at peace. The two slept back to front, the female cradled in the male's arms. Embers glowed softly in the hearth, casting shadows onto their sleeping faces.

Alora inhaled. She knew these two—Saar and Kaelyn—one Stiyaha, one Ursus.

"Show me their recent past." Alora splayed her palm over the water, her fingertips extended. Slowly, she moved her hand in a wide circle, rewinding the events that led these two here, to this unknown place.

The cabin faded. Another moment, the two were in the strongroom at the Keep.

Too far. Alora reversed course, moving forward in time once again. The images slowed. In the forest not far from one of the Keep's manual entrances, Saar removed a blindfold from Kaelyn. *"You're free. Run, little bear, run."*

Alora's pulse rose. He'd let her go. Why?

The water in the bowl bubbled, and a new vision formed. Saar lay sprawled on a wooden floor in a small room, secured by chains. Cuts and bruises marred his skin. The window shattered. Kaelyn jumped into the room and brought her mace down, shattering the bindings that held him in place. In the next image, the two ran through the woods, wet clothes clinging to their bodies, the cabin looming in the distance.

The vision faded, the bubbles calming until the ripples disappeared.

They care for each other...love each other.

Alora stepped to the kitchen counter, her mind spinning. With a quick turn on her toes, she paced in the small space between her visus bacin and the kitchen table.

As part of Alora's last punishment for breaking the rules by assisting her characters, she'd been forced to give her Ursus to Zedron as recompense. They should be loyal to him. If Kaelyn could come around, maybe the others would as well. Alora's chest lightened, her spirit soaring at the possibility.

On the wall above the table, lights from her character board flashed red and green, melding and scurrying around like Dogo bugs on an infested Etila tree. She approached, and goosebumps formed along her arms. With trembling fingers, she swiped her palm over the board, searching the long list of character names.

At long last, she came to the name she wanted—Kaelyn. She pressed her finger against the red light. Her bio flitted across the screen: birth date, species, job title, favorite weapon, number of kills, lineage. Alora focused on the last item, born to Arbane and Entrania.

Ursus royalty.

Alora clapped her hands together, her smile so wide her cheeks ached. Kaelyn was the royal heir, the true leader among the Ursus. Under the stress, Alora had forgotten that detail. If anyone could influence her kind to turn against Zedron, it was Kaelyn.

Maybe, just maybe, Alora had a chance in this war.

She slid her finger to her waistband and tugged Zedron's

recording device free. The small orb glistened in the light, reigniting her hope. She brought the disc to her mouth and gave it a quick kiss. The smacking of her lips echoed in the room, and she giggled. "I wish you were here, Veromé, to share this with me."

She held the small device close to her chest. A thought formed in her mind, and she let the idea build. A zip of excitement skittered along her nerves.

Veromé wouldn't like her approach, but this was her war, and for better or worse, she'd play on her terms.

No risk, no reward.

She glanced out the window. Night still blanketed the trees in darkness, punctuated by the soft glow of the many stars in the galaxy. Good, she still had time. Before she could change her mind, she grabbed her coat from the door hook and raced into the night.

CHAPTER 31

Kaelyn inhaled, and Saar's pepper and lime scent eased into her lungs. His arm, tucked around her waist, was warm and protective. A sense of well-being expanded deep inside, and she snuggled tighter, pressing into his chest. A soft sigh escaped his lips, but he didn't wake.

She opened her eyes. Still warm from the day's fire, a few stray embers glowed in the hearth. One twinkled brighter for a moment, then disappeared, its fire extinguished. Through the slits in the curtains, an orange brilliance lit up the sky—sunset.

Their day of peace was over.

She closed her eyes, inhaling his scent and nuzzling into him once again. Not ready for reality, she held on to the memory of their day together, but time, the ever proceeding soldier, was relentless.

What would they do now? Hunted by both sides of the war, there was no place they could go where they would be safe. All along, she'd known the time they'd spent here in the cabin was temporary.

A vision floated across her mind's eye. Mauree's gleaming eyes as she thrust her dagger into Theron's gut. Kaelyn's pulse rose. Anger, hot and fast, slid along her nerves.

She couldn't, no wouldn't, let Mauree get away with murder.

There had to be a way around Zedron's protective barrier, a way to kill that malevolent bitch.

She had to return. Alone.

Saar would try to stop her, or worse yet, try to protect her. She'd lost enough males in her life, she wouldn't lose him, too.

"Little bear, you're tense. What's wrong?" Saar's deep voice rumbled in his chest. Concern laced his tone, sending a dagger into her heart.

"The sun is setting." She rolled away from him and onto the cold wooden floor.

His hand trailed over her bare back, his touch tender and caring, but he didn't stop her. She refused to look at him, afraid she wouldn't be able to complete her task. With a quick push, she rose to her feet. The loss of his warmth left her cold. Goosebumps formed along her arms, but couldn't match the ice freezing her heart.

She crossed the small room to her clothes and dressed in silence.

Behind her, the ferns rustled. Clothing swished as he put on his pants and boots. "*Craya…*"

Saar's heavy footsteps echoed as he approached. He placed his hands on her arms, rubbing her skin.

She swallowed, willing herself to be strong. The urge to turn and wrap herself in his embrace was almost more than she could bear.

"What is it? How can I help—"

Steeling her courage, she turned to face him. His beautiful blue eyes reflected his strength, his determination, his caring. She couldn't maintain eye contact, and as her gaze drew downward, her attention riveted to his neck. Around his smooth skin two dark bands, like tattoos, encircled his throat. Those hadn't been there last night.

She gasped. "Your neck…"

A flinch crossed his features. "How many bands are there?"

Quick as liquid, a sudden chill raced down her spine. "What's wrong? Are you ill? What can I—"

"How many?" The tenseness in his words took her breath away.

"Two," she whispered.

His shoulders eased, and he cupped her chin in his palm. With tender care, he drew his thumb across her cheek. "Thank the gods."

"What are they?"

A tentative smile curled his lips. "Bonding bands. Two signify a strong relationship. It's part of the bonding process."

"Bonding *process*?" Her mind whirled. "What does that mean, exactly?"

Saar's smile widened. "This happened when I asked you if you would bond with me."

Thoughts freezing, she couldn't process his words. "H...how?"

"As with all males of my kind, I have a bonding sac under my tongue. When you agreed to bond with me, I broke the pouch, and my bonding ink flowed from me to you—"

"So that's what it was. I remember a sudden strong taste in my mouth."

He trailed a finger over her shoulder. "You have a mark, too."

A sudden tightness squeezed her chest. "I do?"

"I wish we had a mirror so I could show you, but you have three dark marks across your shoulder blade that match mine." The look of pure reverence in his eyes melted her on the spot. "I never realized how close in resemblance they were to a bear's claw until I met you."

Her heart soared at the knowledge they were tied together forever. Yet, she had to get away from him.

She glanced to the windows. Through the panes, the sun's brilliant, final rays cast long shadows between the trees. "We can't stay here. You know as well as I that both my kind and yours will pursue us."

"Where you go, I go, little bear." Conviction tightened his mouth.

No. Determination to complete her goal coiled in her gut. She didn't want to hurt him, but the sooner she got this over with, the better for them both.

He grazed his finger down the side of her face.

With more force than she'd intended, she brushed away his touch. "I think it's best if we go our separate ways."

A flinch crossed his face, and his brow furrowed. "I don't understand. After today," he shook his head as he studied her, his eyes flitting back and forth, pain etched inside, "I thought you understood how I…" *…feel about you.* He didn't need to finish his sentence.

He loved her. Hell, he'd bonded with her, disobeyed his king, given up his home, everything…for her. Without a doubt, he'd die trying to protect her, and she would *not* allow that.

I'm such a bitch.

Putting on the best performance of her life, she raised her chin and hit him where it would hurt the most. "You claim to be loyal, but you betrayed Noeh, your king. You gave up centuries of service to him so quickly, all for me. How could I ever trust that you wouldn't betray me the same way?"

He recoiled, taking a step back. His mouth fell open, and a low growl emerged from his lips. A tic started in his jaw. His features hardened, the scar pulling tightly against his skin. The formidable warrior she'd first met had returned. "You are my mate. Do you really think so little of me? So little of us?"

Her chest squeezed around her lungs. She couldn't breathe. Several long seconds ticked by, the air between them thick with tension. A quick glance through the window and into the sunset gave her the courage to finish this conversation and set him free. "There's no future between us. There never was. Leave before I pick up my mace and we return to where we met—at war."

His eyes narrowed, but sadness radiated from him in waves.

"Little bear," his attention drew to her braiding scarf wrapped around his wrist then back to her eyes, "your words are at odds with your actions. Why are you doing this? Why are you pushing me away?"

The back of her throat ached. *I'm afraid to lose you.* In her mind, she screamed the words at him, wanting him to hear her so desperately. Instead, she turned her back on him.

He wrapped her in his embrace, tugging her back against his chest. "You don't have to be tough with me, little bear. I won't leave you, not now, not ever—"

"No!" She wrenched herself from his arms and turned to face him once again. Tension flared the pain in her jaw. "Don't make promises you can't keep!"

He flinched then his features softened. Love, compassion, and understanding reflected in his beautiful blue eyes. "The tough female that's not afraid to battle her enemy at a cliff's edge…is afraid to love."

Her heart skipped a beat. She couldn't breathe, her chest wound too tight.

Before he could stop her, she grabbed her mace and raced for the front door. He followed in hot pursuit. As she yanked the door open, the setting sun's last ray burst into the room.

Saar's scream echoed through the cabin. The distinct smell of burning flesh filled the air.

Kaelyn ran into the forest and didn't look back.

CHAPTER 32

*A*lora stood on the platform outside Zedron's home and tugged her coat tight around her throat. The tree creaked as it swayed, caught in the evening breeze. Leaves rustled. The sound tinkled through the branches like whispered words, audible yet indiscernible.

A few strands of hair had escaped Alora's ribbon, tickling her cheek. She wiped them away and yanked on the Yandora vines dangling from a nearby branch.

Inside the large tree home, three chimes echoed. The slick melody reminded Alora of the smooth operator living within. A sour taste formed in her mouth. Once, she'd fallen for his good looks and ingratiating charm. Thank the stars, she'd seen through his facade before she'd accepted his bonding offer.

Familiar footsteps, assured and firm, echoed from within the home.

On the surface below, an eerie howl filled the night—rhondo beasts. Her gut rolled. How she hated the creatures. She'd lost two friends to the deadly beasts, Bellamy, her best girlfriend, and Mitan, her childhood companion. No one deserved that fate.

The door swung open.

Zedron stood in the entry. Dressed in tailored slacks, an impeccable sport coat, and a fancy silken shirt, he seemed overdressed for the evening, but that didn't surprise her. He'd always loved his fine attire. "Hello, Alora. What a pleasant surprise."

A charming smile tugged at his lips, the one she'd fallen for so long ago. She ground her teeth and peered at his eyes. Piercing blue, they bore into her.

With steely determination, she forced herself not to look away. "Pleasant isn't the word I'd use."

He laughed, the irritating chuckle skating over her nerves. "My, my, some things don't change. You always did state your mind. Come in, please." He extended his arm, welcoming her into his home, his sanctuary.

Raising her chin, she strode past him. His unique scent of warm musk and moon ale filtered into her senses, swirling unpleasant memories like a bad storm. She ground her teeth. Time to get down to business.

He closed the door behind her. With an arrogance enough for two males, he strode to the bar. Carved into racks in the Rolmdew tree's inner trunk, a selection of wines and ales lined the dark wood. He selected a bottle of muldoberry wine, flipped open the latch, and poured the liquid into first one glass, then another. The wine gurgled from the bottle, sending the sweet berry scent into the air.

"This isn't a social call." She crossed her arms.

He smirked. "It could be, if you let it."

"That's a battle you already lost."

The muscles in his shoulders tensed for a moment then relaxed. He gripped the long stems between his fingers, one in each hand, and headed her way. "Please, I prefer not to drink alone."

His blue eyes twinkled, but in their depths was a calculation and assuredness that sent ice into her veins.

Before she could refuse, he handed her one of the glasses.

His fingers grazed against hers, sending a bout of revulsion up her throat.

With a quick dip of his chin, he brought the glass to his lips and took a sip. The diamond stud in his nose accentuated the gleam in his eyes. "Please, have some, then share with me why you grace me with your presence."

"I…" The words wouldn't come through her scratchy throat, so she took a sip of the wine. The sweet nectar washed away the ache and calmed her overactive nerves. She was here to bargain with him. Determination coiled in her gut, and she placed the glass on the edge of the bar.

His eyebrow rose.

Plastering on her best smile, she said, "I come bearing a gift, one you won't like."

He placed his hand over his heart, his trimmed and buffed nails resting against his lapel. "I am honored."

She pursed her lips, her anger rising every time he spoke. He should be confrontational, trying to kick her out, force her to leave. His attempt at hospitality knocked her off her game.

A bead of sweat rolled down her back.

"You won't be, once you see what I have." She slipped her fingers into her pocket and tugged the small recording device free. The disc, resting on her palm, shimmered in the light.

His attention riveted to the object. Lines formed around his mouth. "What do you have there?"

"Don't you recognize it?" She taunted him, aware that doing so was like poking a stick at a rhondo beast. You never knew when it would attack, and the outcome could be brutal.

His unwavering stare bore into her. "Should I?"

"It's yours. Of that, I have no doubt." She strutted to his visus bacin and glanced into the murky water. "Ah, Ram, that poor soul. He really didn't deserve his trip to that rehab center on Earth."

Zedron sipped his wine then placed the glass on the bar next to hers. With slow precision, he ran his finger along the stem. "You must be mistaken. Ram is on the character board where he belongs."

"He is now." She tapped her finger against her lip then pointed to the character board on the wall above his scrying bowl. "Have you ever looked under a character's profile? You know, the details beneath their basic info? There's a whole wealth of history there—things they've done, places they've been, a whole cadre of juicy details."

He snapped the glass in two.

She jumped, her heart pounding.

Wine spilled across the counter. A few drops dribbled over the edge and landed on the polished wood floor, staining the grain. "Where did you get that?"

Forcing herself not to give in to the urge to flee, she straightened her shoulders and smiled. "Maybe you should take better care of your recordings. You never know what might end up in the trash or for sale in a thrift store."

A slow, menacing chuckle reverberated from him. "Well, now. That's interesting since I always keep mine. Perhaps my faithful servant isn't so loyal."

She swallowed. He wasn't stupid. As she'd anticipated, he'd figured it out. Time to go all in. Steeling her courage, she steadied her voice. "I could be persuaded not to take this proof of your deception to the council."

He strode toward her, invading her space. His warm, rancid breath was hot and heavy against her chin, her throat. "Go to the council. I don't care. It would be my first offense. You, however, have no chances left. Why should I bargain with you?"

Bile rose in her throat, but she refused to back down. To piss him off, she trailed a finger along his jaw, taunting him. "Because I know you. You don't want to win by default. You want to defeat me, bring me to my knees."

He gripped her arm. A low growl emerged from his chest. "I want you so much. You drive me insane."

She tore away from his grasp. "I take it you're willing to hear my terms."

He hissed. "I'm listening."

"I want two things. First a character, the Ursus Kaelyn."

He pulled back, studying her. "Why?"

"Unlike you, I care for my characters. One of my Stiyaha, a loyal warrior, has fallen for her. I want them to be together." She raised her chin.

His gaze narrowed, flicked to her mouth then returned to her eyes. Silver flashes of desire darted through his irises. "Your love for your characters will be your downfall. They are mere pawns in our game, and I find it amusing they treat us as gods. What is your other demand?"

"Carine."

The skin on his neck reddened. "Never."

"You will." Alora smiled. "You wouldn't want to lose face in front of Radnor. I know how much you love to impress the council leader."

His hardened features remained in place for a moment. He studied her, and she could swear she heard the gears moving in his brain. After a long moment, he relaxed. A soft chuckle eased from him, but there was no mirth in his tone. "I accept your terms on one condition. You must return my recording device to me before you leave."

Warmth crept into her chest, and she pursed her lips so she wouldn't smile. She gave him a quick nod.

A tic pulsed in his jaw, but he headed to the character board. With a quick flick of his fingers, he flashed through different screens until he pulled up the one for Kaelyn. He pressed on her button and deleted his red color. "You can claim Kaelyn now, she's no longer a part of my team."

Alora swallowed and stepped up to his board. Her pulse raced, the rush of blood making her light-headed. She placed her finger against Kaelyn's chart. The small light turned green. She exhaled, relief tracking through her, flushing the adrenaline from her as quickly as it had come.

Zedron held out his palm. Lines formed around his perfect lips. He was one of the most handsome males she'd ever known and also the darkest of heart. "My disc."

"Where's Carine?"

The tic in his jaw pulsed again. "Carine!" His voice boomed in the small space.

Hurried footsteps tracked across the upstairs floor to the top of the landing. With slow, deliberate steps, Carine shuffled down the stairs. Her focus drew from Zedron to Alora. The lines around her mouth tightened. "Yes, my lord?"

"Come here." Zedron's command burst from his clenched teeth.

Carine's face blanched.

Alora spoke softly. "It's all right, Carine. You're coming with me."

Carine's audible inhale filled the room. She placed her hand over her mouth, and her attention returned to Zedron.

He waved her toward him, his movements quick, impatient. "Come here."

Carine took a tentative step then hurried to obey, running to his side. She bowed low before him. "Please, I—"

He gripped Carine's wrist and yanked her forward. She stumbled.

"Don't hurt her!" Alora grabbed Zedron's arm.

He shrugged her off. "Patience, Alora. I need to remove Carine's tracking bracelet." A vicious smirk tugged at his lip. "We can leave it on if you'd like. I have no problem with that."

Alora huffed. "Remove it."

He gave her a curt nod, his arrogance returning full force. Without dropping her gaze, he placed his thumb over the small display. A soft beep emitted from the device. The bracelet slipped from Carine's wrist and clattered onto the wooden floor.

"Go, you belong to her now." Zedron shooed Carine away.

Carine raced behind Alora. Her trembling fingers gripped Alora's arm.

Alora reached into her pocket and snared the recording device. She held out her fist. With deliberate slowness, she uncurled her fingers and dropped the sphere in Zedron's hand. "A fine bargain."

Before he could respond, she gripped Carine's hand and headed for the door, eager to get her friend home. As she grabbed the door-knob, Alora glanced over her shoulder.

A smug smile tugged at Zedron's lips. "Thanks for stopping by."

CHAPTER 33

*T*here was no sleep today, no, not for Gaetan. He hobbled down the corridor, his cane leading the way. Cane, foot, foot, cane, foot, foot. The familiar shuffle, slower and more painful than usual, had become a constant mantra for him.

"Haelen, do you need assistance?" Quentin, decked out in his full armor—black pants, dark shirt, metal cuffs on his forearms—placed his hand on Gaetan's shoulder. His furrowed brow indicated his concern.

"Thank you, no. I'm fine. Just catching my breath." He forced a chuckle to ease the warrior's mind. With the frantic search for Saar and Kaelyn in effect, just about every warrior in the Keep had their hands full. None of them needed to take care of an infirm male like him.

"Good to hear." Quentin gave him a gentle slap on the shoulder then proceeded down the corridor.

Others passed by, merchants on their way to the market, Jixies with baskets of fruits and vegetables for the evening repast, and countless warriors, all searching for their Commander of Arms.

Gaetan's heart pounded. "Saar, I hope you know what you're doing, my friend."

At last, Gaetan reached the throne room. The double doors, usually closed, were wide open. Voices, some stern, some quiet, melded together, their words indecipherable.

"Oh, Gaetan, Noeh's been waiting for you, yes indeed. Please, come in, come in." Jax, Noeh's personal attendant and one of the many Jixies that assisted the Stiyaha here in the Keep, bowed low. His red locks bobbed around his tiny ears. He seemed more elf-like than ever.

"Thank you, Jax. Your cheerful welcome brightens my day." Gaetan smiled. He'd made it a point to treat Jax with the utmost respect, and the little Jixie regarded him as if he were a blood brother.

"I saved a chair for you, yes, I did. That one, over there." He pointed to the seat across from Noeh's desk.

"Much appreciated. Thank you." He patted the little Jixie on the shoulder and hobbled across the stone floor. Noeh and the three warriors didn't seem to notice him. That was good. He didn't want them to see his struggles. As he settled onto the chair, the pain in his leg eased.

The voices quieted.

Noeh cleared his throat. "Saar and Kaelyn have to be out there somewhere. Continue your search and report back to me if you discover any new information."

"Yes, Your Majesty."

"Consider it done."

"We'll find them."

The three males, swords sheathed and dangling from their belts, exited the room, leaving Gaetan alone with his king.

"Shall I shut the doors? Shall I? Shall I?" Jax held his hands low in front of him, his wide-eyed stare intent on Noeh.

"Yes, Jax. Some privacy would be good. Thank you." Tension radiated from Noeh's stiff shoulders and tense jaw, but his words were kind.

"Yes, yes, Your Majesty." Jax strode from the room and closed the doors behind him.

Silence, golden and pure, filled the space.

Gaetan adjusted himself in the chair. "No luck, I take it?"

Noeh ran his hand through his hair. Longer than normal, a few strands fell around his ears. "Ah, *craya*. Warriors searched every nook and cranny in the tunnels then many areas around the Keep. His trail ran in circles with no sign of Saar or the prisoner."

Gaetan rubbed his knee. "Are you surprised? We are talking about Saar, after all."

A short, pained laugh burst from Noeh. "I suppose I shouldn't be."

"What's your plan?"

"As soon as the sun sets, Quentin will expand their search, lead the team—"

"And what will happen when they find him?"

A slight breeze wafted through the room. Several papers on Noeh's desk fluttered, and one slid to the stone floor, landing like a feather, silent and soft. The temperature dropped, and their combined breaths became visible in the air.

The hair on Gaetan's arms rose. This could only mean—

A blinding light lit up the room. Gaetan covered his eyes. The wind whipped about, pinning him to the chair. His cane slipped from his fingers and crashed against the stone floor.

"*Craya!*" Noeh's irritated voice echoed around the room.

"Hello, Noeh." Soft and feminine, the words slipped inside Gaetan, wrapping around his soul. He recognized that voice—Alora. *My goddess.*

He pulled his arm away from his eyes. There she was, in all her glory, decked out in a sheer dress, the soft material swirling around her ankles. He crossed his finger over his forehead and down his nose in the time-honored symbol and reverence for Lemuria.

Despite the scream threatening to come up his throat, he pushed off the chair and crouched on bended knee. An ache travelled up his leg. He clamped his jaw, refusing to show weakness to his goddess. Above all else, he would honor her in the traditional way.

Noeh bowed low, his hand on his heart. "Alora, to what do we owe the pleasure of your visit?"

"Stand tall, Noeh, Gaetan." She paced to Noeh's desk then turned to face them. A smile tugged at her lips. "For once, I bring good news."

Noeh's shoulders relaxed. "Tell me."

She raised her chin, and her eyes flashed a remarkable shade of silver. "Patience was never one of your values, was it?"

No, but it's one of mine. Gaetan wrapped his fingers around the solid wood of his cane. The light reflected off the sunstone at the tip, bringing his attention to the crack running through the precious stone. His chest constricted, but he pushed off the floor to a standing position. Pain pounded against his forehead, and his vision pinpointed before returning.

Noeh chuckled. "Patience is something I strive for. Now, will you tell us your good news?"

She pursed her lips, but her features softened. "I was able to acquire a new ally. Kaelyn. I believe you know her."

Noeh inhaled, his eyes widening. "The Ursus female?"

Alora nodded and tapped her finger against the side of her lip. "She's with Saar. They are safe for the moment, but I suggest you find them soon. You aren't the only ones searching, of that, I have no doubt."

Noeh took a step forward, toward Alora. "I thought she was on Zedron's team. How can—"

Alora held up her hand. "Have faith, Noeh. She works for me now. Find her and your Commander of Arms. I suspect she could be pivotal in this war."

Gaetan cleared his throat. "I can't imagine Mauree will let her go that easily. She'd kill her first."

Alora focused her pale blue eyes on him. He held her gaze along with the laugh that threatened to bubble up his throat. Was he insane for voicing his concern in front of his goddess? Hell, at this point, if she smacked him dead and returned him to the character board for his insolence, she'd do him a favor. At least then, the pain would be gone.

"The solution is simple. Find Kaelyn before Mauree does." Alora snapped her fingers, and the wind whooshed through the room, taking her along in its wake.

Noeh glanced at Gaetan. "As long as I live, I don't think I'll ever understand that female."

Gaetan sighed, the tension draining from his muscles. "It is not for us to question the logic of our goddess." But he did, oh, how he did.

CHAPTER 34

The reddened, charred skin on Saar's arm throbbed. Sweat beaded on his forehead, and a chill raced over his shoulders. He'd tried to stop Kaelyn from leaving, but the moment she opened the cabin's door, the sunlight had stopped him cold. Good thing it had been sunset, when the sun's rays were at their weakest. Otherwise, he'd be dead.

He ground his teeth as a wave of nausea crested over him. *"How could I ever trust that you wouldn't betray me?"* Kaelyn's words tracked through his mind, followed by his father's. *"Does your loyalty lie with the future king or yourself?"*

Kaelyn had delivered a low blow, hitting on his weak spot, bringing up his insecurities big time. A low, agonized moan filled the small cabin. It took him a moment to realize the sound came from his lips.

"Craya!" He clamped his jaw tight, refusing to give in to his weakness.

With determined steps, he headed into the bedroom to retrieve his sword. The ferns, placed so carefully in front of the fire the day before, were strewn around the hearth, evidence of their time spent together. An ache started in his chest, and he let out a roar. The need to chase after her, protect her from her futile task, burned hotter than the sunburn on his arm.

He wrapped his hands around his sword, sheathed it, and glanced through the window. Dusk. The sun was down. He could leave, track after her. *My mate.* He touched the marking around his neck.

With determined strides, he approached the window. A silhouette of his image reflected in the dirty pane. The dark bands were visible against his pale skin. A mixture of happiness, grief, and anxiety swirled together in his gut, reigniting his nausea. His mouth watered, and he swallowed the bitter taste.

Maybe she was right, he wasn't loyal, wasn't worthy of her. Yet, he couldn't leave her, his need to protect his mate strong, unrelenting.

He turned and headed for the doorway leading into the old cabin's main room. As he passed the fireplace and the ferns gracing the hearth, memories of his time with Kaelyn flooded his mind.

The muscles in his back and shoulders tightened. "I'll find you, Kaelyn, prove my loyalty to you, protect you no matter what." He pounded his fist against his chest. "I vow it."

The words bore inside, intertwining and weaving around his soul. Once given, the unbreakable vow would remain with him for eternity.

He opened the door and inhaled, full and deep. Kaelyn's scent, forever ingrained in his mind, lingered in the air. Energy and determination fueling his muscles, he raced into the forest, eager to win back her heart.

Kaelyn hid behind a large boulder. The wind whipped through her hair, carrying the fresh scent of the ocean along with the pungent smell of Gossum. Bile rose in her throat. The urge to battle welled in her chest, and she palmed the handle of her mace.

She'd anticipated the possibility of encountering either someone from her Tribe, the Gossum, or even a Stiyaha or two on her trek to the lake house, but not so soon. *Damn.* She clamped her jaw tight.

She peered around the large stone. Upwind, along a small path at the edge of the beach, was a solitary Gossum. Never bothering to learn their names, she didn't know him, but she recognized his brown and yellow striped shirt and his red baseball cap. He was one of Mauree's minions. *Good.*

He sneaked down the path, toward her, his slinky gait reminding her of a lizard. She released the clasp on her mace and hefted the weapon into her palm. The familiar, welcome weight provided focus.

When he was close enough she could hear his breaths, she burst from her hiding spot and swung her mace.

He skidded to a stop. A loud hiss eased from his lips. The long length of his tongue whipped from his mouth, narrowly missing her nose.

With a flick of her wrist, she propelled her mace at his face.

He blocked her blow with his arm. Bone crunched. His shrill cry rang in the air.

Footsteps pounded on the path.

Not wanting to get trapped by the trees, Kaelyn sprinted onto the beach. The surf pounded at her back, roaring as if it was in a bad mood. Anger bubbled up from inside. She could relate.

Three Gossum skittered down the path. None stopped to assist their injured comrade.

She raised her mace, whipping it around and around.

The three males surrounded her. Tongues snapping, loud hisses, and sharp chuffs echoed above the ocean's thunder.

She didn't wait for them to make the first move. Using the strength of her inner bear, she swung her mace at the closest opponent. One of the spiked tips connected with his shoulder. He grunted.

The other two took advantage. One snapped its long tongue at her, almost connecting with her chin. The other swiped a long claw at her arm. A long scratch drew blood. Pain flared.

"Stop!" Mauree's shrill voice pierced the din. "Stand down."

The Gossum growled, but gave Kaelyn some distance, moving out of her range. Behind them were several males from her Tribe, along with a few other Gossum, and Mauree.

Kaelyn's muscles stiffened, ready to fight. Here was her adversary, the bitch who'd killed Theron. Kaelyn's fingers slid around the handle of her mace, the need for retribution burning in her veins.

"Well, well. Fancy finding you here." Mauree sauntered forward, the swagger in her step swaying her hips. "Where's lover boy?"

"You killed Theron. I hate you!" Kaelyn spat the words at her.

"Now, now. Theron got what he deserved. No one betrays me and lives. That goes for you as well." A hideous smile lit up her features. With a slow turn of her head, she glanced around. "Now, tell me, where is Saar?"

Kaelyn's pulse rose. "Far away. He's none of your concern."

"Oh, I think he's closer than that. We'll find him, and when we do, he's as good as dead." Mauree trailed her finger over her skirt and lifted the edge, revealing her sheathed dagger.

"No!" Kaelyn swung her mace, faster and faster with each revolution. The whir of the ball competed with the ocean's constant boom.

Mauree glanced at her fingers then wiped her nails on her blouse. "My dear, please. You and I both know you can't hurt me." She smiled and glanced at Kaelyn.

"Kaelynnnn!" Saar's shout broke the air.

Kaelyn's blood froze.

Saar emerged from the trees, his sword drawn, the edges of his hair bouncing as he ran toward her and his death.

Mauree pointed at Saar. "Kill him."

Several of her minions bolted toward Kaelyn's mate.

"No!" Before Kaelyn could think twice about her actions, she threw all her momentum into her movements and launched her mace at Mauree.

Mauree's eyes widened. She ducked.

Instead of a direct hit, the mace scraped along Mauree's cheek. The tip gouged into her eye.

Mauree's eyeball burst from the socket with a loud pop. Blood gushed from the wound. Her shattered scream melded with the sea's roar.

Kaelyn's pulse pounded double time. Confusion flitted through her mind. As part of Zedron's team, she shouldn't have been able to harm Mauree. Something had changed. Perhaps the bond with her mate overpowered Zedron's power over her. Hope, feeble and small, expanded in Kaelyn's chest.

CHAPTER 35

*A*drenaline surged through Saar, feeding his muscles with a spurt of energy. Kaelyn stood on the beach in front of Mauree, surrounded by Gossum. His need to protect his mate drove him forward.

One of the Gossum met him halfway. Saar didn't waste any time. He slashed his sword through the air. The blade sliced through flesh and bone.

A garbled noise emitted from the creature's mouth before the head hit a nearby piece of deadwood with a loud whack. Its body stiffened then slid to the sand in a pile of black goo.

A grunt and the wet snap of a tongue caught his attention. The next opponent approached.

Over the creature's shoulder, a surge of Gossum and Ursus rushed forward, one after another, more than Saar could count.

Dread skated over Saar's nerves, coiling like a snake in his gut. Despite his skill as a warrior, his odds of surviving against so many were slim. He didn't care. He'd defeat them all to protect Kaelyn.

Deep inside, his inner beast growled. *Let me free.*

Saar glanced at Kaelyn. She stood over Mauree, her mace dangling at her side.

Love for her washed over him like a soothing wave, solidifying his decision.

Even as the coil in his stomach tightened, a feeling of weightlessness lightened his chest. On his shoulder, the marking for loyalty burned hot, darkening at his commitment.

"My love, my mate. Survive for me!" He relaxed his fingers.

His favorite weapon slipped to the soft sand. There was only one option left to him, so he released the restraints he'd held on to for centuries, freeing his inner beast.

Aware of its newfound freedom, the beast took hold of his mind. Primal thoughts, dark and hungry, blocked all reason.

Bones elongated. Hair grew over his skin. His pants and boots disappeared beneath the thick mat of fur. He howled, the eerie cry unfamiliar even to his ears. Heavy and hot, his breath heaved from his lungs.

The overpowering astringent smell of his enemy filtered into his nose. A low growl burst from his lips.

"Saar!" Sweet and feminine, Kaelyn's voice broke through the beast's fogged mind.

His beast halted for a brief moment, turning to look at her. Deep pools of hazel, her eyes held tears for him.

Mine. A deep, protective snarl eased from his throat. Nothing would stop him from protecting his female...nothing.

A Gossum jumped on his back. Claws dug into his shoulder, but didn't penetrate through the thick fur covering his hide.

Wet and slimy, the creature's tongue stung him on the ear. Pain rippled down his neck, but that only fueled his beast.

He reached behind him, seized his fingers around the creature's neck and yanked.

The Gossum sailed through the air. It hit a nearby tree trunk at the edge of the forest. The crack of its back snapping echoed into the night.

Another replaced the first, latching onto him like a leech. A third rammed him from the side.

Out of the corner of his eye, a large bear sprinted toward him, teeth bared.

They attacked him from all sides.

He lashed out with his claws, nails ripping into flesh.

He howled, a constant roar bursting from his throat.

Pain in his shoulder flared, then in his knee, as his enemies continued their assault.

He gripped a Gossum's tongue, yanking the organ free from its owner. The creature staggered away.

A bear's claws ripped across his face, opening old wounds.

He punched the beast, a strange sense that the creature was more friend than foe. His opponent shook his head, as if dazed.

Sharp teeth clamped on to his shoulder, tearing into the tissue.

Even as he fought, he searched for Kaelyn. Fear that she was dead seized him, chilling his blood.

There...he spotted her.

She stood over Mauree, her mace twirling in the air.

Relief flooded his veins. She was alive.

He moved toward her, but the opponents kept coming, a relentless tide keeping Saar from her.

A roar of sheer frustration ripped from him.

She glanced his way, and their gazes met. What he'd longed for all his life—love—shone in the depths of her beautiful hazel eyes. His heart swelled even as the crushing blows continued, but she wasn't safe, not yet. He pushed his way toward her, ever relentless, ever determined.

Saar's in trouble. Kaelyn's mouth went dry. In a matter of moments, he'd morphed into his beast. Tall with long, shaggy brown hair and large protruding tusks, power, strength, and fortitude emanated in his every move. Standing on the beach not far from the forest's edge, he battled several Gossum and a few of her Tribe.

She desperately wanted to go to him, but the need to kill Mauree clawed at her insides.

The evil bitch held one hand over her empty eye socket and scrambled across the sand, putting distance between them. She looked like a deformed crab.

Kaelyn twirled her mace. "Stop!"

Mauree didn't.

Saar's roar echoed through the air. Kaelyn's pulse rose.

Gossum attacked him from all sides, the bears getting a claw swipe in here and there. A large cut on his forehead glistened in the moonlight. Blood dribbled down his face. Additional blood on his arms and torso matted his fur.

The ground shook with the pounding of heavy feet. Loud shouts and war cries filled the air. Visible between the trees, males dressed in battle gear dashed toward the fray, swords lifted in the air. An army.

The enemy.

One after another, the warriors emerged on the scene, battling the Gossum and her Tribe.

There were too many. Saar wouldn't survive.

The urge to morph rippled over Kaelyn's skin.

"You better go to Saar. If the Gossum and Ursus don't kill him, his own kind will." Mauree continued to gain ground, moving farther away.

Fear wrapped its cold, icy fingers around Kaelyn's heart. Go after Mauree or help Saar? Indecision tore at her insides, shredding her from the inside out.

She wanted to take her anger out on Mauree for this deadly war that had stolen her brother, her parents, her uncle. Yet, her love for Saar tugged at her, encouraging her to release her hatred and go to him.

Home is with Saar.

Her heart constricted and deep inside, the words rang true.

In an instant, she made her decision. Like a pot boiling over, her anger dissipated into the night.

She lowered her mace and glared at Mauree. "You have a reprieve, at least for tonight."

Before Mauree could reply, Kaelyn morphed into her bear and bolted. She wouldn't let Saar die.

~

Screeee! The familiar ring of Stiyaha swords slicing through flesh and bone bolstered Saar's determination. His kind was here. Whether they attacked him along with the Gossum remained to be seen.

He slashed his large claws across an oncoming Gossum, gutting the thing with one fell swoop. Hot and steamy, the creature's intestines dribbled to the ground. He finished it off with a quick punch to the head. Bones crunched beneath his knuckles.

Saar turned his head. A bear launched itself toward him, its knife-like canines bared. The fighter barreled into him, knocking Saar over. They careened to the ground.

Saar's back hit a rock buried in the dirt.

Air burst from his lungs, and he couldn't breathe.

The animal's sharp teeth punctured the skin at his throat. A gush of blood matted his fur.

He gripped the animal by the neck, but he couldn't get any leverage.

A growl of pure rage and the pounding of running feet reverberated in the air.

The weight lifted from him. A smaller bear tackled Saar's opponent, bringing him down. They rolled across the sand until the larger bear's back crashed into a piece of deadwood. The smaller bear glanced at him.

Kaelyn... He'd recognize her hazel eyes anywhere.

One of his own warriors, Quentin, approached the battling pair. Unwavering intent lined his features. He raised his sword.

Saar's gut tightened.

No! The sound came out a growl.

With one swift move, he leapt to his feet and jumped in the

sword's path. The blade pierced through his thick hide and slid between a couple of ribs.

He stilled. Pain burst inside, stealing his breath.

Quentin withdrew his blade, but the movement only amplified the agony.

A loud whistle pierced the air. The bear Kaelyn battled retreated into the forest, along with the other Ursus and any able-bodied Gossum. Mauree and her troops were gone.

Blood coated Kaelyn's fur on her face, her shoulder, her leg.

Red colored Saar's vision, anger and pain fueling the beast's need for vengeance. A loud roar ripped from his throat.

With a swift backhand, he hit Quentin in the chest. The male flew through the air and landed in a heap at the base of a nearby rock.

Unleashed, his inner beast wanted to race after the bear, tear him to shreds for injuring his mate, but the need to tend to her overrode his need for vengeance. Blood dribbled from his wound, stealing his strength, but he rose to his feet.

She was alive, and that was all that mattered. Deep inside, relief filled his soul, his love for her overriding the pain.

She morphed into her human form, her clothes covering the wounds on her shoulder and leg. Instead of anger and regret—love and acceptance reflected in her eyes.

Even as his lifeblood drained from him, he kept his focus on her.

She hobbled to her feet, and his chest ached to see her in such pain. If she hurried, she still had time to escape.

Saar pointed to the forest. *Run.*

Her eyes widened, and her lips moved, as if she'd shouted at him, but the ringing in his ears was so loud, he couldn't hear anything other than the constant buzz.

Out of the corner of his eye, a flash of light caught his attention. His gaze tracked there. The edge of a blade whooshed toward his head. His last thought—*at least she has a chance.*

CHAPTER 36

Kaelyn pushed away from the log, forcing her legs to bear her weight. The salty air held the distinct aroma of blood and war.

Saar.

Kaelyn's chest ached, her love for him spilling from her as freely as the blood flowing from her battle wounds. He'd taken the sword intended for her, proving his loyalty. She knew what that meant to him.

Instead of fear and anger at his sacrifice, a mixture of gratitude and love swirled inside, cementing the bond between them. Love was about caring for others, letting them inside, holding on tight. She'd opened up, allowing herself to care, to become vulnerable, and now, she wouldn't let him go.

Saar struggled to maintain his balance, but his gaze met hers, his eyes full of devotion. He raised his hand and pointed toward the forest. His intent was clear—run.

No. She wouldn't leave him.

The male Saar knocked to the ground stood. The muscles in his shoulders flexed as he picked up his sword. Faster than she thought possible, he raised his weapon.

"Stop!" Kaelyn bolted, plowing into the male and knocking him off balance.

"Ahhhh!" With a soft thud, the blade drove into the soft sand at his feet.

Saar growled, his shoulders flexing, hackles rising on his back. He turned toward the male.

Kaelyn rushed to Saar, colliding with the hard muscles of his chest. Warm and wet, blood from his wounds seeped into her skin, the coppery tang coating the back of her throat.

"Kill him!"

"He's a danger to us all. Kill him!"

Loud shouts and pounding feet reverberated off the nearby trees. Saar wrapped his arm around her waist. He took a step back, toward the forest. His growl was low, menacing.

"Saar, stop." She pushed against him, fighting to break his hold.

From the corner of her eye, a male skirted around them, then another, their swords gripped tightly, faces drawn.

If the Gossum and Ursus don't kill him, his own kind will. Mauree's words flitted through her mind.

Saar wavered on his feet, the blood loss taking its toll. She pulled back and this time, he released her.

She raised her hands toward the warriors. "Don't hurt him."

"Who are you?" One of the males with a bandana wrapped around his throat took a step forward, his sword raised above his head.

"I'm his mate. Kaelyn." Saying the words strengthened the connection between them, solidifying it in her heart.

The male who'd spoken held out his hand. "Move away, Kaelyn. We can protect you."

Her face heated, anger flaring within. "I can bring him back."

"No one..." His voice trailed off. The tension in his arms relaxed, but he didn't lower his sword.

Saar growled and pressed against Kaelyn's back, drawing her to him once again, yet the strength he'd possessed before was gone.

"Others have and you know it. Let me try," she choked out the words.

"Let her try, Quentin," one of the other males shouted.

The warrior, Quentin, glanced at the other Stiyaha and pointed the tip of his sword at the ground.

She didn't wait to see if they followed suit. With a quick turn, she faced Saar and gripped his face in her palm. Even in his beast form, his scar ran from cheek to chin.

He growled and jerked from her grasp, the beast in control.

"Shh...shh...it's okay. They won't hurt you." She brushed a finger over his broad shoulder.

His attention darted from the males to her and back again several times, as if assessing whether to believe her words. At last, his blue eyes rested on her.

She stroked his fur, whispered how much she loved him, anything to keep him with her.

His eyelids drooped then popped open, focusing on her once again. His knees wobbled, and he leaned on her before straightening. Several moments ticked by, but at long last, he closed his eyes.

"That's it, concentrate on my voice. I love you, Saar. Come back to me."

Shuffling of feet and soft murmurs echoed around her, but she focused on Saar, continuing her efforts, stroking his fur, keeping him grounded. She poured all her love for him into her tone, trying to ease the beast within. Then, like a bright light bursting in her mind, she gripped her whistle and brought it to her lips. After taking a big breath, she blew into the bear's head, playing a soft tune, just for him. *Come to me.*

His fur tickled her hand, retracting so slowly she almost didn't notice. The movement bolstered her confidence, her heart beat picking up speed. She continued her quiet melody. His fur receded, his bones and muscles creaking as he reverted to his normal height. Rough, callused skin and his clothes reformed onto his body, including her golden yellow scarf wrapped around his wrist.

He opened his eyes.

A strangled cry eased from her throat. She kissed him on the mouth, firm and hard. He wrapped his arms around her and drew her to him, returning her kiss with a fevered intensity. After a long moment, she pulled away. Their combined panting echoed between them.

With a tenderness she'd grown accustomed to, he trailed his finger over her braid. "Little bear, thank you."

Quentin stepped forward. "Welcome back, Commander."

Kaelyn placed her hand on Saar's chest. "Your injury…"

He raised his shirt. A thick line, a scar, marred his chest. He smiled, the small dimple she loved so much forming in his cheek. "Seems the beast heals quickly, I'd forgotten about that. Looks like another souvenir, a memory of what's important in life."

He cupped her cheek in his hand. His thumb trailed over her chin, and he stroked her like only he could.

She smiled. "It's beautiful."

He brushed his fingers over her shoulder and wrapped his arm around her waist. She leaned into him, a weightlessness lightening her chest.

Quentin cleared his throat. "Noeh sent us to find you, bring you back to the Keep."

His attention riveted on Quentin. A tic started in his jaw. "What are the charges?"

"Charges?" Quentin blinked. "None. On the contrary, he's thankful you did the right thing. Alora visited, said Kaelyn is on our side now. Saar, I tried to save Kaelyn, not hurt her when you hit me."

"What? I'm back on Alora's team? Good thing it's night and I found out before daybreak. Otherwise, I'd burn from the sun." Kaelyn's mind reeled. Her life had changed so drastically in such a short amount of time. "Why didn't Alora tell me?"

Quentin shrugged. "Welcome to the team."

"What about the rest of my kind?" Hope for the others rose in her chest.

"As far as I know, just you."

A cold chill slid along her arms, an awareness she might not see her Tribe again, except on opposite sides of the war.

Saar drew her closer. "We must go. Who knows if Mauree and her troops will return anytime soon. Besides, we need to see Noeh."

"The nearest portal is this way." Quentin and the other males headed into the forest.

Kaelyn followed Saar's gaze to the ocean. Memories of their encounter on the cliff brushed against her mind. She ran her hand down his arm, over her braiding scarf at his wrist, and squeezed his hand. "Maybe someday we'll come back and visit."

He wrapped her in his embrace and tugged her close. His breath cascaded over her chin, stroking her skin. A low, possessive growl rumbled in his chest. "Mated to you is my dream."

Joy lifted her spirit as his lips met hers. She'd found her forever mate, and a happiness she'd never known swelled in her chest. This was love, and she embraced it with all her heart.

CHAPTER 37

*A*lone in her bedroom, Mauree stared at her reflection in the mirror. Red and swollen, her eyelid stretched over her empty eye socket. Along her cheek, a long gash marred her skin. The scratch would heal, but there was no way her eye would grow back.

She picked up one of the many bottles of perfume gracing the dresser top and heaved the vial at her grotesque image. The mirror shattered, bits of glass cascading over the dresser's surface and onto the floor. Like run away marbles, shards skittered over the polished wooden floor.

She turned her back on the vision and gripped the dresser's edge. Her fingers tightened on the wood until it creaked under the pressure.

Vengeance seeped into her cold and bitter heart, hardening the organ into something unrecognizable. "Kaelyn, Saar, Noeh…you will all pay."

There was a soft knock on the door.

Irritation flared her anger. "What?"

Eldon stood at the doorway, his hands crossed in front of him. "What are your orders?"

She pushed away from the dresser and approached him.

He took a step back.

"Look at me," she demanded.

He shuffled his feet then straightened his back and looked into her eye. "Yes, my lady?"

She studied him, her one eye tracking over his body. With a quick smile, she reached for him, wanting to trail a finger down his face, but her depth perception was off. Instead, her hand landed on his shoulder.

Heat flushed through her body, racing up her throat and into her cheeks. "How many troops did we lose?"

"Not as many as I would've expected. Altogether, five Gossum and one Ursus." His attention never wavered. Good thing. If he'd dropped his gaze, she would've gutted him with her knife.

"At least that's something." She huffed and walked back into her room. The first rays of the dawn rose into the sky, glinting off the few shards of glass that remained of the mirror.

Without stopping, she strode to the sliding glass door and opened it. The morning breeze cooled her heated skin, and she closed her eye, enjoying the brief reprieve.

Eldon approached her from behind, but didn't invade her space. Neither spoke for a few moments.

"How long do you think we have until they arrive?" Her words came out harsh.

"A night at most. Do you want to move on, search for another place or stay here, dig in, and fight?"

Good question. The muscles in her arms and legs ached, and a migraine pounded behind her eye. *I'm so tired of running.* "We stay. Let them come."

"Then I will lead your army." His voice was low, determined.

She turned to face him.

He raised an eyebrow. "Is that not what you want, what you need?"

"I need..." She clamped her teeth to the point of pain. From the beginning, she'd longed to exact revenge on Noeh. She cleared her throat. "...to defeat Noeh and win this war."

His features hardened, resolve forming behind his dark eyes. "When that happens, I'll be right by your side."

She nodded. "Yes, you shall."

～

Veromé's molecules recombined, coalescing into his physical form. Alora inhaled, and Veromé's salty and fresh scent wafted into her senses. Before she could greet him, his arms wrapped around her waist, and he drew her against him. Her hands landed on his chest, and she ran her fingers over the firm muscles in his broad shoulders.

"Hello, my love." His voice reverberated deep in his chest. The vibration travelled all the way to her toes.

She peered at him through her lashes.

He smiled, creases forming around his beautiful blue eyes. A streak of gold flashed through his irises, teasing her into wanting something they couldn't have—more time together.

"Veromé, I've missed you, as always." She kissed him, enjoying how the small hairs of his goatee teased her chin.

He planted kisses along her neck until he reached her ear. His breath tickled her skin, sending a shiver all the way down her spine.

He pulled back to look at her, cupping her cheeks in his palms. "Tell me, my love. What did you do with Zedron's disc?"

A knot formed in her stomach. She withdrew from his embrace and strode to her visus bacin. The smooth, still water was calm, so unlike the nerves spiraling inside her.

Over Veromé's shoulder, through the carved opening in the Rolmdew tree, dawn's rays painted the clouds a vibrant red. There was no point in putting off the inevitable. He'd find out one way or another, probably sooner rather than later.

She wheeled to face him, her bottom pressed against the counter for support. "This won't make you happy, but I bargained with Zedron."

"You did what?" He pinched the bridge of his nose and exhaled. "Tell me the rest."

"I saw Kaelyn in my visus bacin. She loves Saar. If she can cross over to our side, maybe the others can as well. I went to Zedron—"

"Do *not* tell me you gave him that disc." The sharp, bitter tone of his voice made her flinch.

She thrust out her chin. "So what if I did?"

"Alora, that was a stupid mistake. Don't your realize—"

Her face heated. "Don't you call me stupid."

He huffed. "I'm sorry, my love, but I fear you don't realize how devious he is. He'll use that against you. You should've gone to the council."

She scoffed. "How could he possibly use this against me?"

"The council may see your unwillingness to bring charges against Zedron as manipulation. Along with the fact you bargained with him?" His tone lowered. "That could be construed as coercion which could lead to another sanction."

Fear slid over her nerves, toying with her. No wonder Zedron had given in to her demand so easily. She picked up the vase of Coletta flowers from the table and launched them at the wall. The vase shattered, bits of glass scattering across the floor.

"Alora, calm down." Veromé enfolded her in his embrace.

A thought struck her. She pulled back, trying to force the anger racing through her veins to slow. "Wouldn't Zedron be sanctioned for cheating by preventing Ram from returning to the character board?"

His features softened, but the worry in his eyes persisted. "Most likely, but it would only be his first offense, whereas, yours would be…"

"My third. I'd lose the war," she whispered.

Would he turn her in? If he wanted to, without a doubt.

An uncontrollable shiver wracked her body.

The stairs leading to the second floor creaked. Carine peered down at them from the top step. "I don't mean to interrupt, but…"

Veromé stilled. "Carine? What are you doing here?"

The Arotaar female proceeded down the stairs.

Alora left Veromé's side and draped her arm around Carine's shoulder. "She's staying with us. I bargained for her as well."

Veromé let loose an exasperated breath. "Alora, you shouldn't have done that. Zedron has something up his sleeve, I'm sure of it and—"

The first rays of the morning sun appeared, sending Alora to her dark place. Her resolve hardened. Zedron had upped the stakes in their war. If he wanted a fight, he'd get one.

CHAPTER 38

Saar gripped Kaelyn's hand and led her down the corridor. The sunstones lining the Keep's walls glowed, casting soft shadows over her features. He peered at her. The dark strands of her braid shimmered in the subdued light. His chest expanded, love for her filling him with a happiness he hadn't known before.

A sexy smile tugged at her lips, her brow furrowing. "What? Do I have a crumb on my chin or something?"

He chuckled, and the sound blended in with their boots clacking as they strode down the hall. "You're beautiful, and no, there's no crumb. Stop worrying. You'll be fine."

She flipped her braid over her shoulder. "I can't help it. I want to make a good impression. It's not every day you meet a king."

This time the laugh erupted from him, echoing down the hallway. "Says the Ursus queen."

She bumped her shoulder against him. "Quit. I'm not that here."

"You can't change who you are, Kaelyn." He stopped in front of Noeh and Melissa's chamber. "This is where they reside."

When they'd arrived in the Keep, Saar had contacted Noeh through the sunstones. The king had asked them to stop at his private chamber instead of meeting him in the throne room. What would Noeh think of him?

Quentin had said no charges would be brought against him, but he wouldn't know where he stood until he saw Noeh's face.

A bead of sweat dribbled down Saar's cheek. He wiped it away with the back of his hand then rapped his knuckles against the wooden door's fine grain.

Kaelyn inhaled.

He squeezed her fingers, giving her as much support as he could, which wasn't much, given the circumstances.

"Come in." Melissa's soft voice slipped through the cracks around the frame.

Saar gripped the handle and turned the knob. The door opened on a soft whoosh. Warm air caressed his skin, and another bead of sweat tracked after the first. He stepped forward, leading Kaelyn into Noeh and Melissa's private chamber.

Melissa stood close by. She wore a blue and green satin dress, the colors of the royal family. "Saar, so glad to see you."

Her attention tracked to his throat. A knowing smile graced her lips. She gave him a quick hug then glanced at Kaelyn. "You must be Kaelyn. I'm so happy to meet you. Welcome. I hope your previous encounter here didn't mar your impression of us."

Kaelyn shook her head and glanced at Saar. She smiled, that beautiful smile he'd grown to love. "No, my memories are good ones."

Saar's heart soared, but he didn't have time to dwell on it.

Noeh stepped from the hallway that led to his private bathing chamber. Dressed in a pair of silken pants and a hand-woven, button-down shirt, he ran a towel over his short-cropped hair. A drop of water glistened on his chin, evidence of his recent bath. Their gazes locked.

A knot formed in Saar's gut, curling into a hard ball.

Noeh's features softened. "Saar."

The king approached.

Saar bent down on one knee. "Your Majesty, I—"

Noeh placed his hand on Saar's shoulder. "Rise, my good friend."

Saar rose. His heart pounded loud in his ears. He'd spoken without thought, forgetting that Noeh couldn't hear him. He met his king's gaze and tried again. "Your Majesty, I ask for your—"

Noeh held up his hand. "Stop, Saar. No apologies. You did the right thing. Kaelyn is our ally. Had you killed her at my command…" A shudder visibly wracked his body. "Your choice may have saved us all."

Choice…the word rang like a bell in Saar's mind along with Kaelyn's words. *"He chose to go with you, didn't he? You aren't responsible for his choice."*

Years ago, Saar had made a decision, one with long-lasting ramifications. If he hadn't asked Noeh to stay to watch the bucks, he wouldn't have put his friend in jeopardy. Saar had carried the guilt with him for years, but in the end, Noeh had elected to stay.

Life was all about choices and consequences, and he wasn't responsible for someone else's actions or decisions. The guilt that had plagued him because of his father's words lifted from his shoulders. His scar tingled, and his marking for loyalty burned on his shoulder. He didn't need to see the line to know it darkened.

Saar turned to Kaelyn. "Noeh, I want you to meet Kaelyn, queen of the Ursus, and my mate."

Noeh's gaze tracked to Saar's throat. "So I see, and a good bonding as well." He returned his attention to Kaelyn and took one of her hands, capturing it between his palms. "Welcome, Kaelyn, Ursus queen. We are thankful you're here."

Kaelyn smiled and gave him a quick bow. "Thank you. It is my pleasure and an honor."

Melissa placed her hand on Noeh's arm. "Okay, that's enough formality. I'm so excited for the two of you. Congratulations on your bonding."

Saar's chest expanded, and he pulled Kaelyn into his embrace. "Thank you. I'm blessed."

Kaelyn's smile widened, and he wanted to kiss her until they ended up all tangled in some sheets in one of the guest bedrooms. There was no way they'd make it back to his quarters, not at this rate.

Noeh ran his hand through his short hair. A few wet strands

remained upright. "One other thing. I hear you shifted and returned. How did you…"

Saar glanced at Kaelyn. She smiled, her eyes twinkling with affection.

He swallowed the lump forming in his throat and choked out the words. "I'm not entirely sure, but Kaelyn brought me back. She talked me down with her soothing voice and with the melody from her whistle. With her help, I was able to reconnect the strands linking me to my beast."

Noeh inclined his head toward Kaelyn. "Do you have an "M" in your hand?"

She blinked. "What?"

Melissa held out her palm. "If you look closely, you can see the outline of an "M" in my hand. Sheri and I have them. We're both human, and we helped our mates shift back from their beast forms. We believe the mark stands for "Mu" which is short for Lemuria. Do you have one, too?"

Kaelyn held out both hands. Her palms were clear, unblemished. "Doesn't appear so."

Noeh wrapped his arm around Melissa's waist, pulling her close. "Perhaps, then, it has more to do with the mating bond."

Melissa's brow bunched together. "But why do Sheri and I have these identical marks?"

Noeh placed a soft kiss on his queen's forehead. "Between Gaetan and Tanen, we hope to find an answer soon."

An eerie quiet from the antechamber caught Saar's attention. "Is Anlon asleep?"

Noeh cleared his throat. "Gaetan is watching him for a bit."

Melissa glanced at Noeh, a grin forming at the corner of her mouth.

Saar put two and two together. "Uh, I think it's time we left."

Noeh winked. "Good idea."

Saar didn't need another hint. "As you command."

He gripped Kaelyn's hand and turned to leave.

"Welcome home, my loyal friend." Noeh's words eased into Saar.

He faced his king once again and bent to one knee.

Noeh placed his hand on Saar's shoulder, stopping him. He chuckled. "Leave, my friend, before I kick you out."

Kaelyn wrapped her fingers around her braiding scarf at his wrist and tugged. "Let's go." She leaned in and whispered, "I want some alone time with you, too."

His heart swelled. He was home, free of his guilt and happy for the first time in his life. His love for Kaelyn overwhelmed him, expanding his chest to the point of pain. Faster than he thought possible, he drew her from the room.

Once outside, he captured her in a dark part of the corridor, trapping her between his body and the wall. Slow and deliberate, he trailed kisses up her throat until he reached her ear. "Is this what you want?"

"That will do for a start." She laced her hands behind his head and kissed him, hard.

He growled, the sound drifting down the corridor.

As he'd predicted, they didn't make it to his quarters.

CHAPTER 39

*G*aetan trudged around the corner and into the Portal Navigation Center. The scent of pine trees and dampness filtered into his senses. Quentin, the lone warrior in the room, sheathed his sword. His gaze flicked between Gaetan and Anlon, perched in the crook of Gaetan's arm.

"You starting the training? I didn't realize Anlon was ready." Quentin's shirt had several dark stains, no doubt Gossum blood from the recent battle.

Anlon struggled in Gaetan's embrace, arms and legs squirming in all directions.

Gaetan leaned down and set the little prince on the floor. Pain shot up his leg, and like a bad case of trailing ivy, it wrapped around his muscles, squeezing the nerves tight. Jaw clenched, he spoke through gritted teeth. "We're starting early and giving Noeh and Melissa some private time."

"Ah, I understand now. I'll leave you alone with Rin and Anlon." Quentin chuckled and slapped Gaetan on the shoulder on his way out the door. The movement jolted Gaetan, and he held his breath.

"Ya okay? Yer lookin' kind'a pale there, chief." Rin wiped his hands on a rag.

Over his shoulder, a slight mist, the final remnants of the portal, swirled on the platform. Information about the last battle, the one on the beach with Kaelyn and Saar, had travelled through the Keep like wildfire.

"I'm fine, thank you." Gaetan hobbled to Rin's solitary chair situated near his workbench. He leaned his weary body against the seat, easing some of the pressure from his leg.

The little Jixie wiped a cloth over the sunstones lining the porte stanen, the giant stone that ignited the portal. His fingers, gnarled from arthritis, worked the cloth between each stone, rubbing and polishing with a reverence and love only he could give them. As the Portal Navigator, Rin's job was to maintain the portal, make sure it was operational at all times. He took his job very seriously.

That was why Gaetan had come here. Maybe, he'd have an extra sunstone that would fit Gaetan's staff.

Rin peered at him, the red in his goatee a shade darker than the short tufts on his head. He tilted his head. "What can I do for ya?"

Gaetan held up his staff. "My sunstone cracked. Do you have a spare?"

The little Jixie cringed. "Ah, ya know 'tis bad luck to crack one."

"Yes, I know. Can you help me out?"

Anlon crawled over to Rin and tugged on his leg. The small male smiled and tussled the newbs hair. "Hello, little prince."

Gaetan's heart expanded, swelling with pride. Everyone loved Anlon. The prince, as the sole child in the Keep, brought hope to so many within its walls.

Anlon plopped into a sitting position. He raised his hands and one of the stones from Rin's workbench floated through the air straight for the child, as if carried on an invisible string. Anlon plucked the red stone from its course. A soft giggle, full of wonder and happiness, burst from him.

Rin chuckled. "I'd give ya that one, but I think Anlon jus' claimed it."

"Indeed, he did." Gaetan adjusted himself on the seat and leaned against his cane, letting the rod take his weight.

"Well, let's look and see what we can do for ya." Rin approached Gaetan and tossed his rag onto the workbench. The cloth landed on several small gems, hiding them from view. Rin held out his hand. "Let me take a look at yer staff."

The thought of putting weight back on his leg didn't sit well with Gaetan, but he adjusted himself, bearing down on his sore leg. He handed his staff to Rin.

The small male studied the stone, turning the rod this way and that. "I've got one for ya. It's over here—"

The central portal stone brightened, deep red bathing the walls in shades of blood. A loud whoosh followed by a stiff breeze blew through the room. Mist swirled over the portal's platform, more than had been there before.

The skin on Gaetan's arm tingled, never a good sign. "Anlon?"

A small child-like giggle reverberated off the walls. Gaetan glanced toward the sound.

The young prince crawled toward the portal, his hands and knees trekking across the Keep's stone floor faster than Gaetan thought possible. The bitter taste of bile filled his mouth. There was no way he'd get there in time.

"No, oh no!" Rin inhaled. Gaetan's cane slipped from his fingers and bounced against the stone surface. He bolted for the portal.

Anlon crawled up the two stairs leading to the platform. Mist swirled in a ball, growing larger with each of Gaetan's heartbeats.

Gaetan's breath stalled, his lungs unable to move, pinched by his tight chest.

The young prince slipped into the mist, disappearing before their eyes. His soft giggle echoed from within the vapor. In an instant, the fog dissipated.

"Anlon!" Rin stumbled over the stairs. His hands landed on the platform, sprawling, searching. The little Jixie turned to face Gaetan, his brow furrowed, his features grim. "The prince. He's gone."

Gaetan stood without the aid of his cane. He hobbled to Rin as fast as his deformity would allow. "What were the last coordinates?"

Rin rushed to the porte stanen and studied the stones. Fear etched deep lines around his eyes. "I don't rightly know. He could be anywhere."

Dread, cold and hard, drew its fingernails down Gaetan's spine, finding his knee and digging in deep. He welcomed the pain. This was his fault. Noeh and Melissa had placed Anlon in his care.

Alora, please, dear goddess, watch over the little prince, watch over us all.

SNEAK PEEK - CLONE ME A LOVER

INTERSTELLAR LOVERS BOOK 1

Forbidden to express emotions, clone Angelo Thirteen longs to experience one feeling above all others—love. When a tenacious, young, female Altonian retrieves him from his drifting space pod, he may just get his chance.

Chapter 1

Angelo Thirteen rolled the stone in his palm, but its smooth, cool surface couldn't calm his racing heart. He was almost to Iridis, almost…free. A sense of giddiness lightened his chest as he studied his precious piece. Silver lines in the stone's crevasses refracted the spaceship's artificial light, sending a cascade of brilliant radiance against the ship's console. With a fevered intensity, he clasped his fingers around his lucky rock—the one that helped him escape Earth's oppressive, tyrannical rule.

A soft, electronic ping returned his attention to his pilot duties. He glanced at the vid-monitor. The screen displayed a red world, swirling dust storms raging its surface. *My new home.* Angelo Thirteen's breath caught in his throat, and he kissed the rock before placing his prize on the ship's console.

"Arriving within Iridis's orbit in eighteen minutes, thirty seconds." Mortimer's deep voice resonated through the cockpit. The ship's computer was as much a part of the crew as the terraformers in the central bay.

"Setting coordinates for a rendezvous with the base colony now." Chad Seven, the ship's co-pilot, swiped his fingers across the screen, his deep blue eyes void of emotion.

Angelo Thirteen's pulse pounded in his ears. Didn't his co-pilot have any sense of wonder? *No. That was a forbidden emotion.*

In 2364, hatred, bitterness, and prejudice started the *Last War*, culminating in a biological attack that left few survivors on Earth. Out of the aftermath, the remaining leaders joined forces and created *The Accord* which laid down several laws, including the suppression of all emotions. To replenish the diminished population, the members of *The Accord* cloned themselves, each identical replica receiving a successive number. Angelo Thirteen touched the tattoo on his cheek, the one just under his eye—13. The raised numbers, rough against his skin, forever marked him. He ground his teeth.

At age twenty-eight, he was one in a long line of Angelo clones bearing the same dark brown hair, brown eyes, and consistent five-o'clock-shadow stubble. Like those before him, he was conditioned not to feel, not to express emotions. Although he didn't know what made him different, he longed to be an individual.

Angelo Thirteen leaned back in his chair. Cold, bitter steel from the chair's neck rest grazed against his skin. Goosebumps formed along his nape. He wiped his fingers over the lumps and flicked a small switch, opening a ship-wide channel. "Everyone, this is your pilot Angelo Thirteen. We are approaching Iridis's orbit. Prepare to disembark in thirty minutes."

As pilot of *Wanderer*, his responsibility was to transport eight terraformers, water creation equipment, food and medical supplies to Iridis. Fortunately, Iridis offered Angelo Thirteen an opportunity. Not only had he collected the unusual stone from Chad Seven in a poker match, he'd also won his co-pilot's lottery ticket—the one for the job of maintenance technician on the base. Good thing Angelo Thirteen met the requirements—three years in the shipyards and two years in *The Bungalow*, the electronics academy. But...there was a catch. If Angelo Thirteen didn't perform to standards, he'd be shipped back to Earth and its restrictive, emotionless rules. A chill ran over his arms.

He shut off the link, picked the stone off the console and glanced at his co-pilot.

Chad Seven raised his chin. "I'd like the chance to win back my stone."

Angelo Thirteen repressed a smile. "I rather like the bauble. Which planet did you say it came from again?"

"Transinia, in the Cassiopeia constellation. I won it in a poker game from a Trolog. He wasn't happy to lose."

"I'll bet. Perhaps you'll get your chance later, but for now, I'm keeping it." Angelo Thirteen raised the stone to the light, entranced as the fine flecks of silver shimmered. With a quick move, he pocketed his treasure and pointed at the bags of coffee under Chad Seven's seat. "Besides, you still owe me from the last game. If I liked coffee, I'd take some of that in payment."

"Fat chance. This is the best coffee in the galaxy. By the way, I had to relieve my pent-up frustration in one of the copulation clubs because I lost to you." Chad Seven's eyes darkened. His lip curled at the corner for a brief moment before his face resumed his stoic pose. "At least they know me well there."

Angelo Thirteen swallowed through his tight throat. Everyone was required to attend on a regular basis as the government feared without the sexual outlet overwhelming emotions could lead to another war. At least sexually transmitted diseases and pregnancy were no longer an issue due to medical advances and egg harvesting. The copulation clubs were a means to an end, but he longed for something more...something special, intimate, and enduring.

Chad Seven coughed. "When was the last time you went to one?"

Angelo Thirteen tensed, the muscles in his shoulders clenching beneath his shirt. He forced a shrug. "A few months ago. I go once in a while." *Only to avoid hitting the government's radar for non-attendance.*

"Come with me next time. I'll introduce you to some of the regulars." Chad Seven's lip twitched ever so slightly.

"Naw, man. I'll pass."

"Suit yourself." Chad Seven gripped his hand around his liquid container. The smooth, semi-sheer material expanded, molding to his palm. "Before we transport the passengers and materials to the surface, I'm going to refill my coffee cup. I'd ask if you want any, but…"

Angelo Thirteen shook his head. "Just be back in time. We enter Iridis's orbit in ten minutes. I don't want to do this on my own."

Wanderer was built as several detachable pods all linked together, each one a separate room. Fortunately, the galley was in the adjacent pod.

Chad Seven stood, placed his hands on the small of his back, and stretched. Joints popped loud in the enclosed space. He gave a quick nod, ran his hand through his short blond hair, and exited through the small hatch. His steps echoed down the hall. As with all the rooms in *Wanderer*, the imitation gravity field kept them grounded.

Alone for the moment, he glanced at Iridis in the vid-monitor. His heart expanded. How he longed to be free, allowed to settle on this new planet, one without Earth's oppressive rules. Here, the residents had established their own government, *The Coalition*. Emotions were not only allowed, but welcomed. A sense of giddiness overwhelmed him. He couldn't wait to land.

Angelo Thirteen tapped his finger against his armrest and peered at the digital display. Five minutes had passed since his co-pilot left to refill his coffee cup.

C'mon, Chad Seven, where are you? A sense of unease rippled over his shoulders.

Mortimer's deep voice broke through the silence. "Entering Iridis's atmosphere. Unidentified object in flight path. Suggest evasive—"

A firm shudder vibrated through *Wanderer*.

The ship lurched, rolling into a forty-five degree angle.

Angelo Thirteen careened from his chair and skidded across the cold metal floor. His shoulder crashed into the bulkhead. Pain radiated down his arm.

Flashing lights lit up the console.

The shrill peal of an alarm filled the air.

Down the hall, screams echoed from the passengers.

Angelo Thirteen's heart raced. "Mortimer, assessment."

"Something hit the ship. Structural damage in pod nine."

Pushing against the metal wall, he struggled to stand. A quick glance at the vid-monitor displayed a large piece of metal floating past *Wanderer*, remnants of some other ship's broken hull. *Space garbage.* His good luck had run out.

His stomach clenched. "Mortimer, can you fix it?"

"Negative. Full containment breach in thirty seconds."

A ball of fear formed in Angelo Thirteen's gut. Would they all die? Concern for his crew tightened the coil in his gut. He gripped the edge of his chair. *Wanderer* flipped upside down and continued its slow roll. Screams intensified.

"Mortimer, disengage pods in twenty seconds."

He stretched toward the console. With the tip of his finger, he flipped on the com switch. "Crew! Pods will disengage in eighteen seconds. Secure yourself in the nearest pod and close the hatch. Prepare for launch."

Down the hallway, Chad Seven gripped a com unit attached to the wall. As he tried to pull himself toward the bridge, the muscles in his face contorted, his lips white with strain. Angelo Thirteen's throat constricted. His co-pilot wouldn't make it here in time.

Angelo Thirteen waved him away. "Go with the terraformers. Now!"

Chad Seven blinked once. His lips pursed then he disappeared into the galley.

A quick breath escaped Angelo Thirteen. At least his co-pilot was in one of the pods.

"Ten...nine..."

Pulling himself along, he reached the hatch.

"Eight...seven..."

He tugged on the firm metal. The door wouldn't budge.

His heartbeat pounded at his temple.

"Six...five."

With a shot of adrenaline coursing through his veins, he yanked on the handle. Screeches emitted from the hinges as the door closed.

"Four...three."

The seal engaged with a soft whir.

"Two...one."

A loud clank sent a shockwave reverberating through the ship. Angelo Thirteen glanced at the vid-monitor. Four pods descended toward Iridis. He let loose a loud sigh. His crew would be safe.

"Fire in backup generator." Mortimer's voice sent a chill down his arm.

"Extinguish it—"

An explosion shook the pilot pod. The vibration knocked Angelo Thirteen against the bulkhead. White dots formed in his vision. An insistent ping resonated from the console—the oxygen warning. Something warm and wet dribbled over his brow.

The ship's artificial gravitational field gave out. His boots lost contact with the floor, and he floated into the middle of the room. He couldn't concentrate, his mind a jumble. Yet, his gaze pulled to the vid-monitor.

Iridis shrank into the distance.

His chest constricted. Drifting in space, he faced his worst fear...he was alone. His vision tunneled, and he focused on his lost world, his lost hope, until the darkness engulfed him.

For more information on *Clone Me a Lover*, visit www.rosalieredd.com.

ALSO BY ROSALIE REDD

Books in the *Warriors of Lemuria* series:
Untouchable Lover - book #1
Untamable Lover - book #2
Unimaginable Lover - book #3
Unforgivable Lover - book #5 - **Coming 2018**
Unforgettable Lover - novella
Alora's Love Potion - short story collection
Marked by Love - novella

Reviews

Enjoyed *Undeniable Lover*? The best gift you can give an author is an honest review. Please consider leaving a review on your favorite retailer to help spread the word and support an author.

Newsletter

Want access to free reads, special offers, and giveaways? Sign up here for my newsletter on my website and you'll receive a **free ebook**. Don't worry, your information won't be shared with anyone but my muse. You can visit me at my website at www.rosalieredd.com or contact me at Rosalie@rosalieredd.com. I love to receive email from readers!

GLOSSARY

Arotaars: People from the planet Arotin. Held as slaves on Lemuria. They have blue hair that sparks with electricity when they are emotional.

Craya: An expletive.

Dren: Short for "chil*dren*." Originally human adults, but were transformed into Dren through a Lemurian's bite. During the "turning," all Dren receive a unique, special power. Dren must drink blood at least once a week from the opposite sex or they become weak and lose their powers.

Gossum: Human converts turned by another Gossum through their bite. They have black eyes, and are hairless, with rough, scalelike skin down their neck and back. Gossum have a spur at the end of their long tongue which they use to paralyze their prey.

Haelen: Healer

Jixies: Small, dwarf-like characters that voluntarily serve the Stiyaha. Jixies tend to be quick, resourceful, and are great planners. Despite their short stature, they can go amongst the humans to obtain special items not made within the Keep.

Keep: The underground home of the Stiyaha and Jixies, located in the mountains of the Pacific Northwest. The Keep is sentient and reacts to her inhabitants with minor tremors and/or by warming or cooling the environment through the sunstones embedded in the walls.

Lemuria: A planet in the Orion constellation. Lemuria is slowly dying and its people must rely on natural resources from other planets to survive.

Lemurians: Refers to both the people on Lemuria, as well as, the characters on Earth. The people of Lemuria appear as gods to the characters in the war on Earth.

Newbs: Young children

Panthera: Sleek and muscular, these highly skilled fighters are known for their speed and agility. They transform into black panthers and are highly arrogant and confident. They respect strength and cunning and will only follow a leader who can command them.

Porte stanen: The massive stone structure in the Portal Navigation Center used to transport characters in and out of the Keep through the portal gateway.

Rhondo beasts: Fearsome creatures that terrorize the surface of Lemuria. They have black, oily skin with disproportionately long arms and short legs. A small amount of hair runs down its spine. They have a long tongue and sharp teeth, including tusk-like fangs.

Stiyaha: Stoic and just, Stiyaha are noble warriors. Tall and strong, they transform into large beasts, between eight and nine feet tall, covered in fur with large, protruding tusks.

Sunstones: Magical stones that line the ceilings and walls of the Keep, providing heat and light to its inhabitants. Sunstones are used in trade and have some healing abilities.

Ursus: A tough, burly species that shape-shifts into large bears. Tenacious and vicious, they are fierce warriors.

Visus bacin: Scrying bowl

Yandora vines: A trailing plant the lives on the bark of the Etila trees. The leaves have a melodic tingle when touched.

ABOUT ROSALIE

After finishing a rewarding career in finance and accounting, it was time for award-winning author Rosalie Redd to put away the spreadsheets and take out the word processor. She pens paranormal, science fiction, and fantasy romance in her office cave located in Oregon, where rain is just another excuse to keep writing.